THE
HERMIT
BOY

THE HERMIT BOY

IDA CHITTUM

ILLUSTRATED BY
JAY RIVKIN

DELACORTE PRESS / NEW YORK

Text Copyright © 1972 by Ida Chittum
Illustrations Copyright © 1972 by Dell Publishing Co., Inc.
All rights reserved. No part of this book may be
reproduced in any form or by any means without the prior
written permission of the Publisher, excepting brief
quotes used in connection with reviews written specifically
for inclusion in a magazine or newspaper.
Library of Congress Catalog Card Number: 77-180923

Manufactured in the United States of America
First printing

Library of Congress Cataloging in Publication Data

Chittum, Ida.
The hermit boy.

SUMMARY: During their summer vacation in the Ozarks,
two girls befriend a mysterious boy
who lives alone in the woods.
[1. Friendship—Fiction. 2. Ozark Mountains
—Fiction] I. Rivkin, Jay, illus. II. Title.
PZ7.C4453He   [Fic]   77-180923

1660471

TO

J. R. C.

CONTENTS

THE
HERMIT
BOY

1. THE TRIP

Samme turned from staring out the window to face her older sister.

"I like taking a bus trip. Are there any bears in the Ozark Mountains?"

"Still a few, I believe."

"Wolves?"

"Gray timber wolves."

"Wild deer?"

"Oh yes."

"Snakes?"

"Of course. Lots of snakes."

"Poison snakes?"

Since Edith was thirteen years old and read constantly, Samme had faith in most of her answers. "When Aunt Rose came to see us last summer, remember, she told us that the hills were thick with copperheads. Copperheads are poisonous snakes, related to the water moccasin and the rattler." Samme groaned. "I couldn't care less about their relatives. Aunt Rose said she uncovered a nest of young copperheads just in front of her house along a stone fence." Edith leaned against the seat. "No good in worrying ahead of time. Just relax and enjoy the trip."

The yellow bus stopped in front of the diner. "Twenty minutes," said the driver.

The girls headed for the lunch counter. Samme began digging in her purse for nickles and dimes. "I'm going to buy some candy bars to eat between stops— makes me feel rich." She looked over the different kinds of candy. Edith ordered hamburgers with everything. A box of real-looking plastic lizards took Samme's thoughts back to the earlier conversation. "I wish I had a snake bite kit."

"Please," Edith said, frowning. "Don't mention snakes for a while. At least not until after we eat. Okay?"

"Okay."

By the time the hamburgers and cokes were finished the driver was heading for the door.

Edith stood up. "Time to get on the bus."

Samme followed her sister, gazing all the time into the well-filled paper bag. A dozen assorted ten cent chocolate bars, two pieces of fudge and four purple gumdrops.

"Look at them." She held up a purple ball. "The size of a walnut."

"They do look good. Let's get our seats."

They were just settled when the bus lurched forward. Samme took a firm hold on the back of the seat and, stretching, pushed the precious brown paper bag of candy onto the luggage rack overhead.

"Someone else has lots of things up there, too."

"Of course. We aren't the only people on this bus." Edith smiled.

"Horses! Horses!" Samme cried happily.

Edith shrugged. She didn't feel as strongly about horses as her sister.

"Look, look!"

"I'm looking. I'm looking."

"What's that?"

"What's what?" Edith leaned over her younger sister, staring out the window. "Where?"

"Not out there," Samme said, nudging her sister. "In the bus. What's that noise?"

"*Snort, snort, ka, ka, ka, frume.*" The sounds came in waves.

"It's coming from the seat in back of ours."

Trying to be discreet, Edith turned slightly. Samme turned around and took a good look. "He's snoring."

"*Snort, snort, ka, ka, ka, frume.*" The choking sounds rattled up and down the aisle, filling the bus.

3

"Wow!" Samme said with a grin. "I thought we'd blown a tire."

Farmland rolled by. Small towns snapped into view and disappeared. They counted the houses along the highway. The tenth one was to be the house they would live in when they got married. Samme wouldn't play again when her tenth house turned out to be a converted cowshed.

The snorts and ka, ka, ka, frumes still came from the tired man slumped in the seat behind them.

"That Mr. Ka Frume," Samme said, giggling, "isn't seeing much of the landscape."

Coming into another small town, the bus slowed and stopped before a drugstore.

"Oberville," the bus driver called, looking back. No one stood up. "Oberville," the driver repeated louder.

The snoring just behind the girls continued. The driver came down the aisle and shook the sleeping man.

"Your stop, sir. You wanted off here, sir."

The tired man struggled to his feet. He began tugging at the luggage overhead. A blue valise hit the floor with a thud, followed by a large package that burst open. Square white soda crackers scattered over the floor.

Edith helped gather scattered ties and socks. When she sat back down, it was on two tuna fish sandwiches. There went her hope of keeping clean for two-hundred miles. What good did it do to look clean if you smelled like tuna?

The thin, tired-looking little man tossed together

4

what seemed to be the last of his possessions, apologized and stumbled off the bus.

"Hey! Hey!" Samme shouted. She made frantic motions to the bus driver. "That man left his leg."

The astonished driver turned around.

"His chicken leg. He left it." She waved the part of the man's lunch that had settled in her lap.

The driver looked relieved and started up the bus.

Samme put the chicken leg in a bag for scraps under her seat.

She closed her eyes and pretended to snore like Mr. Ka Frume, only not very loud.

"All right. Act like Mr. Ka Frume. Snore if you want to," Edith said. "But don't knock all the bags down when you wake up."

It was two hours and quite a few towns later when Edith woke Samme up.

"This is it. Our stop. The town nearest to Aunt Rose's house."

Their heads close together, the girls stared out the open window. The building before which the bus stopped was the color of winter smoke. A team of mules with glistening black coats pulled a wagonload of freshly cut logs around the yellow bus.

The driver took their bag from the rack overhead and led the way down the bus steps. Samme clutched the bag of candy.

"You girls have a nice summer."

The big bus, their recent nest, pulled away in a cloud of exhaust fumes. They were alone.

"We're still twenty-five miles from Aunt Rose's

house." Samme clutched her purse and the candy. She looked suspiciously up and down the deserted street.

Edith tried to tidy up by brushing down her thick, brown hair. "All we have to do now is telephone that neighbor."

Samme brightened. "We are to use the phone at the ice-cream store, and wait. I like to wait in ice-cream stores."

"So there is nothing to worry about." Edith continued. "I hope."

They found the store and looked in. A woman, her hair rolled in a tight knot, was standing behind a wooden counter. As they entered, she smiled in a friendly, curious way. "You girls looking for someone?"

Edith pulled a carefully saved paper from her purse. "We just came in on the bus."

The woman nodded, waiting.

"We would like to use your phone to call the Groves. William T. Groves."

"They'll come in to pick us up," Samme chimed in.

"We're going to stay this whole summer with our Aunt Rose. She asked Mother if we could. Mother said being out-of-doors in the summer is good for people. Aunt Rose lives 25 miles out in the hills."

The woman clasped her hands together. "Twenty-five miles. Oh, you poor, poor children."

Both girls' eyes widened in alarm. Then Edith was calm again. She must not let Samme, who was only ten years old, see she was worried.

"If we could just use your phone." She stared at the

wooden box with the black horn, no dial. She had seen pictures of phones like that. You just turned the crank to get the operator.

"If you only could." The woman turned to the telephone. "The line's out. Bad windstorm last night. Be days before they get it fixed."

The girls felt their hearts sink. Edith thought hard. Samme found two dimes for ice-cream cones.

"Anyone we can hire to drive us out there?" Edith asked.

"Lots of townfolks don't know the way." The woman pondered the problem. There was a clatter as an old truck came to a stop before the door. She jumped up. "Hold on, here's Henry. He's acquainted out that way some. Maybe he'll take you."

A lanky, disheveled, dusty man pushed his way into the door, grinning. He raised a cloud of dust when he sat down on a stool.

"You know the way out past Lamb's country store to the Groves?" asked the woman as she handed him a glass of water.

"We have to get to our Aunt Rose's," Samme said.

Henry nodded. "For a double ice-cream cone, I reckon I'd know. Your aunt, eh!" He drank the water at one gulp. "Rose Shaw, isn't it? Practical nurse. I've heard of her. I have some kin out that way, they've mentioned her. Came to the hills some years ago for her health."

"She's the nurse-lady lives all alone out there in the timber," the woman addressed Henry.

"Yes, ma'am," Henry answered. "Think I can find

my way out there. She fixed up the old Given's place, mile down the creek from a big empty house. Can't take you right to it, girls. Right soon they're opening up a new county road out that'a way I hear, not quite ready yet."

Visions of being stranded disappeared. The girls cheered up. Edith took three one-dollar bills from her purse. She laid them before Henry on the counter. "Do the best you can," she said. "I guess we can walk a mile." Samme nodded eagerly.

Henry picked up two of the bills. "You girls keep that one. Stuff yourselves with ice cream and candy. May be a long while till you see either again, goin' that far back in the hills."

The woman followed them as far as the door, smiling through the screen as the girls thanked her and embarked on the last lap of their journey into the Ozarks.

Henry tossed the suitcase with a "clunk" into the back of the truck. He tugged the stubborn door open and the girls climbed in. Henry fitted his long legs under the steering wheel. They rattled to a one pump gas station. Henry held up two fingers to the attendant. The gas in, he turned to the girls. "All set?"

They nodded. "This isn't a bit like the bus," Samme said, "but we're glad you're taking us."

"Then let's aim for the country, girls."

With many protests from the motor they were off. They bounced across a twin set of railroad tracks, then past a row of deserted sheds, scattering dogs and chickens at the edge of the village.

8

At first there were a few small farms, then log houses with hounds in the yard. These gave way to stretches of open country, stony hills and valleys. The bouncing truck hit an extra deep rut. Henry drove intently, gripping the wheel and aiming for a narrow bridge. "Made it," he announced as they leapfrogged over the vibrating planks. A sheer cliff loomed before them.

For a frightening second it seemed that they must plunge straight into the wall. But with a deft turn of the wheel Henry skirted around it. "Made it again," he yelled proudly. "Done 'er a hundred times."

The girls were grateful.

"Hold on, girls, the road gets rough here."

Edith gasped. She already felt as if they were riding in a churn. Her hair had all the beauty and daintiness of a well-used dust mop. She ventured a look at Henry. He seemed calm, so she relaxed. This was a mistake because the truck struck another deep rut and the girls flew into the air. Their heads hit the roof with a "thunk" and down they came in a cloud of dust.

"Folks have to hang upside down around here to dig a well," Henry shouted. It was one of his hill jokes. "Kids raised here grow up with one leg shorter than the other from walking around the hills." He was full of them!

Henry bent over the wheel, coaxing the truck up the steepest hill yet. The truck gasped and stopped. There was a tense pause, a gigantic chug and they were on top of the hill. As they balanced there dangerously, Henry said, "That way to the old empty house."

He pointed down, so far below that the trees looked

the size of matches. "There's the country store." The girls strained their eyes, feeling that they were about to see one of the wonders of the world. What confronted them was a box building with a row of mailboxes along the front. The truck gasped again and they rattled down the long hill, bombed by pebbles.

For the last few moments they had not been thinking of arrival, but survival. Now they understood why Henry was the color of dust. They might have been two dust-colored sisters of dust-colored Henry.

"Hold on, girls, we turn here."

The truck twisted as if it would snap in two. They spun off the road onto a narrow trail. They leaped two deep ruts and hit the third straight on. Nosey branches pushed into the truck's window. They were in the woods now, and it was cooler. There were heavy scents of stunted dogwood, decaying leaves and rotting logs, dried mushrooms and new May apples. Reaching vines threatened to drag them from the seat.

"Old Indian trail," Henry said.

"I wouldn't be surprised to see a crowd of old Indians still using it," Edith groaned.

At last they were in a clearing. A gaunt, three-storied house loomed before them.

"Good grief." Samme eyed the old house. It looked unfriendly.

Henry guided the truck along a narrow track between the house and a leaning barn.

"Down there's a creek."

He shut off the motor to save gas. The truck coasted,

never missing a rock or a root jutting from the lane. They bumped to a stop before a swift flowing, silver-colored stream.

The girls jumped out and stood beneath a majestic oak. Its giant bouquets of leaves, reaching skyward, seemed to welcome them to Summer Valley.

2. ARRIVAL

Henry climbed down from the truck. "Journey's end," he announced. He went to the water's edge, thrust his face into the stream and drank. He raised a dripping chin. "Pardon me, ladies, for going ahead. There's a tin in the truck. I'll get it for you." He fished around under the dusty seat and pulled out an empty juice can. "There you are!"

Edith shook her head. "Think I'll drink out of the creek the way you did."

Samme agreed. "I have a feeling that can is the truck's drinking cup."

"Right you are." Henry poured water into the radiator. "She's dry, too."

"Look, animal tracks." Samme almost stuck her nose in the creek sand. Silver water beads hung from her chin.

Henry sauntered to the water's edge. "Coon. If you look at the big trees close by, you will find one has a hole in it. Look at the bark, you'll see gray coon hairs. Then you've got yourself a coon tree."

"A coon tree I couldn't use." Samme stood up and brushed sand off her dress.

Henry prepared to return to the village. "Just follow the creek that way," he said. "If you get lost, just do the way city folks do."

"What's that?" Samme asked.

"Holler up the holler," Henry said with a grin. He climbed back into the truck. Samme and Edith gazed after him wistfully as the truck chugged away.

Good old Henry. Gone forever. It was a sobering thought. Their last link to the world of people.

"Poor, poor us," Samme mourned. "Lost and gone forever no doubt, like my Darling Clementine." She closed her eyes, opened her mouth and began to scream.

The birds flew away, squirrels scattered, Edith

13

jumped. "Why are you screaming? You scared me to death."

"I'm lost. I was just hollering up the holler like Henry advised. I wish I had a snake bite kit. I wish I had my nose over the lunch counter back home with a hamburger in my hand," Samme complained.

"Have a candy bar," Edith said.

"Ah good!" Samme reached into the brown paper sack and pulled out a piece of fudge. "Am I hungry. This sure looks good. Have some."

"Thank you," Edith said. "Well, let's get up the creek." She tramped ahead.

They rounded the curve in the stream and were up against a giant fallen oak. Samme straddled the log and refused to move.

"Not in those deep vines I won't," she said grimly. "Snakes could be hiding down under those vines, hundreds of snakes!"

"I'll help you." Edith took a long stick and pushed it back and forth and up and down, stirring the vines. "Now! It's okay," she said comfortingly. "Absolutely free of snakes."

"Thanks a million, Sister. Someday I'll do as much for you." Samme slid off the log and stood up. The grass ahead stood tall and thick. An easy breeze blew back and forth, making the whole meadow flow with yellow green waves.

Edith pushed back some fuzzy willows. "Looks like we're in a pasture."

Samme's eyes widened. "You mean a pasture where cows live? I'm almost as afraid of cows as I am of

snakes. Cows just stand and look at you. Like this!
Sometimes they come right at you, too." Samme drew
her lips thin. "I'd never have gotten off the bus if I'd
known."

"They only want to be fed when they do that."

"Just the same I'm glad that cows aren't meat eat-
ers." She pushed on into the tall grass until Edith
couldn't see her at all. Then a deep sigh reached
Edith's ears. "It's no use. I can't walk in this tall grass."

"Tell you what," Edith said, "let's try walking on
the other side. We'll cross."

"Shoes, socks and all?" Samme asked doubtfully,
looking down at her feet.

"Pull them off," Edith said, sitting down to remove
hers.

The icy, silver, rippling water circled their knees.
The girls stood facing a red clay bank higher than
their heads. They tossed their shoes and the bag of
candy thankful that they landed safely. With a mighty
struggle, reaching her hands high, Edith with Samme's
help placed the suitcases beside the shoes.

"Now to get ourselves to the top." Edith took hold
of a stout branch. She pulled herself upward, pushing
bare toes in the sticky clay. There was a squish! She
slid back the same distance she had climbed.

"Try this one," Samme said, catching hold of a
longer branch.

At last the girls were up on the bank beside their
belongings, looking somewhat the worse for the ex-
perience.

"Let's put our shoes and socks on the first thing. We

must look like two drowned rats," Edith moaned. "But look, at least here's a path."

"That's a path?" Samme studied the faint trail.

"An animal path." Edith shrugged her shoulders. "We must follow it. There isn't any choice."

The sun streaks along the valley's edge were fainter. The path lay deep in shadows and the shadows were becoming darker by the minute. After they'd walked a long distance the path began to slant, diving down into a mass of tangled grapevines.

"So we've come to the end. What do we do now?" Samme looked at her older sister and guide.

"We bend way down," Edith said. "See where the path leads? We're lots taller than possums."

But at last even this trace disappeared, ending in a marsh circled with flat white stones.

"Possums didn't lay these stones," Samme said.

Across the marsh the creek widened. A thick log had been put across the creek.

"So true," Edith said. "And possums didn't lay this log bridge."

Samme let out a shout that made Edith start. "Nor build that nice house on the hill. See! See that house in the trees."

It was the very picture Aunt Rose had sent. All those windows. French windows she had called them. Built them in herself.

In their joy and excitement Samme and Edith started off on a run.

They ran right into the reed-covered marsh. "It's a

trap," Samme protested, for the mud nearly claimed both her shoes.

Edith pulled herself onto a wide smooth rock. "Come on." She tugged Samme's hand. "We will know enough to walk around swamps the next time."

"Need a few sidewalks around here." Samme scowled at her mud-covered legs.

Making their way out of the soggy ground and carefully placing one foot before the other like tightrope walkers, they were able to cross the log bridge without mishap.

On the other side was a wider path which wound past a spring and continued up the hill.

As they neared the house, an army of cats appeared. They gathered around the girls in a furry, tail-waving framework, curious and not quite friendly.

"This just has to be Aunt Rose's house." Edith knocked on the door panel. No answer. She touched the door, it opened. They stepped into a long room. A third of the room where they stood was the kitchen. The other two thirds made up the dining space and living space. Near them was a low stand with a water bucket and a dipper. A hook on the dipper handle kept the dipper from slipping down into the pail. Beside this was a white enamel basin and two folded towels. A few feet across the room was an iron cooking stove, polished and gleaming. It stood just far enough out from the wall to allow room for a long woodbox. To the left a tall white cupboard reached to the ceiling. The dining room area contained a black enameled round table and four matching, shining chairs.

Black-and-white rag rugs lay before large open-armed chairs along the end of the long room. The sides and end of the room were lined with French windows identical to those at the front of the house.

Summer Valley, which spread out below the windows, was full of shadows. Edith took in the whole scene. "Samme, isn't it just like a picture from a magazine, Samme? Samme, where are you?"

Samme came out of one of the doors which opened off the long room. She had taken off her wet clothes and put on a zebra-striped flannel robe.

"What will Aunt Rose say?" Edith cried.

"She'll say I had the good sense to change to something dry. Here's one for you." Samme pushed a roomy gown of black cotton toward her sister.

"I just hope this *is* Aunt Rose's house," Edith said, laughing. She could see over Samme's shoulder out the window. Her hand flew to her mouth and the laughter stopped. "Someone's coming! A man!"

Samme didn't turn. She was afraid to look.

Edith shaded her eyes, the better to see. "He's carrying something. Something alive. And in the other hand he has an axe."

Samme snatched two sticks of wood from the box behind the iron stove.

"Prepare to defend yourself," she said, thrusting a piece of the wood into Edith's hand. She whirled her own weapon in a wide circle.

"Careful, you almost hit me," Edith said.

She pressed her nose against the glass. "He's on the path."

Samme's stick of wood hit the floor with a "thunk." "He's almost here." Samme moved close to her sister. "Imagine us in such a fix. Alone deep in the mountains. Night coming on, in a house that belongs to no-telling-who and a stranger sneaking up the path."

"He's carrying a pig under his arm," Edith whispered.

She pulled Samme away from the window. "Let's sit down at the table. Act nonchalant."

Without a knock, the door opened. The cats could be seen in the background, a semicircle of lashing tails and watchful eyes.

A weathered man, soft-footed as the cats, stepped into the cabin. He and his clothing blended into one hue as if both had been out together in the rain and sun many times. His cracked shoes left bits of brown, broken leaves on the polished floor. The black-and-white pig which he carried squirmed as he lowered it to the floor. The pig, its tail wonderfully curled, began an unguided tour of the kitchen.

The man leaned the axe, which he carried in the other hand, against the wall, Samme sighed with relief.

Now he turned to the girls. Putting his hand to his high-crowned, shapeless hat, he raised it six inches above his head in a wordless greeting. Replacing his hat, he began searching every pocket, bringing from them rough, black walnuts. He made an orderly pyramid of them by the door. When the job seemed finished and the many pockets empty, he went through them all again.

He turned a weathered face to the girls. Then he lifted the felt hat up and down three more times, and walked out the door.

Samme came alive first and ran to the door. "Your pig," she shrieked. "You forgot your pig!" Her words rose, swelled and faded in the treetops. She turned back to Edith. "I tried, didn't I? You can't say I didn't try."

"I won't," Edith vowed, wiping her forehead. "I'll never say you didn't try."

"Tomorrow that same man will no doubt return. He'll enter without knocking, raise his hat three times, pick up that pile of walnuts, put this pig under his arm, then he, pig, nuts, axe and all will go out the door into the trees," Samme said. They both laughed.

"Never to be seen again," Edith finished.

"Look," Samme shrieked. "The cats are running away. Deserting!"

And as they watched, the last of the army of cats, a frail, yellow bit of a kitten, his tail sticking straight out, raced down the path. . . .

3. GRANNY MAY'S CABIN

After seconds the cats came back. In the center of the cats was Aunt Rose. The girls ran to meet her.

Aunt Rose hadn't changed one bit since she had visited in the city. She was a dried-apple doll of a woman. Small and vigorous, her eyes were dark like Samme's and always smiling. Her gray hair was parted in the middle, drawn back smoothly and wound into a secure bun at the back. "Girls." She hurried forward in a wave of purring cats.

"Are we glad to see you." Samme swept along the path in the flowing robe.

"Thank goodness you've arrived!" Aunt Rose exclaimed. "I was worried when I didn't get the expected call, then there was another emergency. The neighbor over the ridge sent for me. The stork waits for no man. When they need help the neighbors call on me but I don't mind."

She hugged and kissed each girl.

"It must be handy for the people out here having a real nurse about." Edith smiled. "Maybe I will be a nurse when I grow up."

"My." Aunt Rose looked the girls up and down. "You've grown so. I see you've found something comfortable to change into. How did you get here?"

"Henry brought us," Edith said, "as far as the old house."

"Then you had to walk along the creek. The new county road will be opening soon. It runs closer to my house," Aunt Rose said. "I must thank Henry." She held up the yellow kitten. "Have you met the cats? This is Butterball. This striped mother is Bee Bee. There is Boris named for his black mustache. The big fat tom is named Pillow Paws. See his big feet?"

Edith laughed. "Pillow Paws is my favorite."

"I love them, every one." Samme hugged her aunt. "And especially I love you. Those cats scared me to death. They all ran away."

"My welcoming committee. So very sorry I couldn't be here when you arrived. Well! To the house. Light the lantern and off to the spring for milk."

"You keep your cow at the spring?" Samme asked.

Aunt Rose laughed merrily. "There's no cow. I buy milk from the Groves. Then I put it in tin pails which I keep in spring water. The milk keeps for days. Spring water is icy cold. What's that, a pig?" She turned to Edith.

There was no need for an answer. The pig was banging around at the woodbox.

Aunt Rose touched a wooden match to the wick of a lamp.

"Oh!" Edith shrieked. She had stepped right into the pile of nuts. One leg went east. The other leg went west. Edith went down. The piglet came running, grunting to see if someone was serving supper. "And —and here is the pile of nuts that came with the pig."

"And there is a large nut on top of the others," Samme said, grinning. "And I don't mean that innocent pig."

"Here," Aunt Rose said, "is a bag to put them in. The Baron has been here, right?" she asked.

"Didn't say what his name was," Edith said, tossing the mound of black walnuts into a paper bag.

"Why did he leave his pig in your house?" Samme asked, frowning in wonder. Aunt Rose lifted her thin shoulders. "The runt of the litter very likely. Me being a nurse, he figures I can take better care of it than he can."

"Looks strong enough to me," Samme observed.

"As far as putting the pig in the house. That's the way the Baron lives. What he's used to. The Baron lets his animals live in as well as outside. Strange as it may seem the animals prefer the outside just as he does, for he lives out most of the time himself. Only in snow or hard rain does the Baron retreat into the shelter of a shingle roof. Well, we can take care of this little fellow. There's a small pigpen over near the barn empty right now. Built with a small loft over it, too, handy for storing the corn."

Edith shook her head. "If the Baron lets the pigs run in and out, he certainly can't be a very particular housekeeper." She tossed the last nut into the sack.

Aunt Rose slid the thick glass globe back into place and handed the glowing lantern to Samme. "I'll lead the way." She scooped up the touring pig. "Edith, you bring the sack of nuts. The loft above the pig's pen is dry so we can store the nuts there as well as corn. That's the way it is in the country. Everywhere you go there is something to carry. When you return there is another article that needs carrying back."

They went out the door. It was dark. Aunt Rose in the lead started down the path. Samme walked in the middle with the lantern. Edith brought up the rear, and the cats were everywhere, their furry legs making giant shadows, flashing back and forth, eerie in the sketchy light of the lantern.

When they were back in the neat house, the girls were perfectly willing for once to rest while Aunt Rose set out a bowl of red-polished apples, new carrots, then proceeded to place a hot supper before them. When they offered to help she smiled. "There will be plenty of helping out when you are rested. I am sorry I couldn't be here when you arrived."

"You couldn't help it if the wind came along and blew down the telephone wires," Samme said.

Aunt Rose poured the cocoa. She set the butter before Samme's plate. "Have another bun."

"Ummm!" Samme spread the butter and added a topping of wild grape jelly.

"There are no houses except that tall empty house on the far hill."

Edith looked at her gentle aunt. "Do you ever get lonely?"

Aunt Rose smiled. "Never gave it a thought," she said. She kissed each girl on the cheek. "I'm so happy to have you. The sunshine and fresh air will do you good and it is such a joy to have company. Now to bed."

"It's a good thing." Samme grinned sheepishly. "Honestly, I can hardly keep my eyes open."

With her arms around both girls, Aunt Rose led them into the room she had prepared.

The next morning when Edith woke up she was staring out at a fat squirrel staring in at her. The sun was bright and laid a silver path across the floor from the open door. The huge oak, that was the scolding squirrel's castle, grew within arm's reach of the door.

"Hey!" Edith shouted.

Samme groaned. "Turn off that television."

"That's not television. That's a squirrel making that funny noise. I think he was scolding."

Samme turned over in bed. "A squirrel on television?"

"Wake up. We are at Aunt Rose's house in the woods. Remember! Look up in the tree out there. It's a real squirrel and has a family."

Samme sat up blinking. The blinking turned to a stare of astonishment as four miniature red squirrels appeared out of a hollow in the tree. They joined in the noisy scolding the older squirrel was giving the girls. Samme flung back the covers, leaped out of bed and ran to the doorway, her hands outstretched.

"I almost had one," she cried.

"Never," Edith cried. "They zipped away. Let's get dressed."

Moments later the girls passed through the kitchen and out the door. Summer Valley shimmered, in a dew-sprinkled, sun-touched opening just below them. The house was perched just halfway up the steep hill. The girls looked down the hill and up another across the valley.

On many of the smaller trees clustered grapevines grew downward, forming green leafy tents as they touched the ground.

Sun and shadow vied for space. Overhead, birds fluttered and fussed. Butterflies floated past, insects strange and familiar were on the move underfoot, and even the velvety moss seemed alive.

"To think there's no one within miles but us. Us and Aunt Rose," Samme said.

Edith was deep in thought. She looked away into the depths of the forest. "I wonder how it would be, way out there, late at night, standing alone under a full moon."

Samme gazed off into the endless trees, imagining wolves howling, owls hooting and bats . . . "Say where *is* Aunt Rose?"

There was the scraping of wood. Their aunt was just closing the latch of the pig's pen. "Come look," she called. "See him eat. Reminds me that I'm hungry, too." They watched as the pig kept his nose in the morning mash. "How about hot cakes for us?" Aunt Rose asked. "Have to go to the spring first, and there are jars of honey in the cellar."

With a clean pail, Aunt Rose dipped into the spring for water to take to the house for drinking. Edith reached in and out, oh, so fast, for the bucket of milk that sat in the bottom of the spring. Samme reached in for the smallest bucket that held the butter. "Brrrr, if you let your hand in for more than a second, it just begins to freeze." To get into the cellar they went around the outside of the house, entering the door there. It was built into the side of the hill and under the house. Bright light poured in from the south window, which looked down on Summer Valley.

"I let the door stand partly open this time of year," Aunt Rose said, "and a pair of orioles nest here each summer."

The nest, a brown bag six or seven inches deep, hung from the rafters, almost in the center of the room.

"A soft, cozy, swinging cradle for oriole babies." Reaching up, Aunt Rose touched the bag gently. "The parent birds line the nest new each year with grass, hair and wool. You'll soon get to know them; the male is bright orange and black, the female is not so brightly colored."

"Must be many nice things in the woods," Edith remarked, thinking of the jars of wild honey.

From a row of golden jars Aunt Rose selected one, handing it to Samme.

"Yes, many nice things. Many interesting experiences may be enjoyed, by taking one's time and walking in the woods."

Their aunt went to another cupboard. "See the jars. Blackberry jams and jellies as well as many quarts of berries canned whole for pies. People could gather blackberries by the wagonload along the edge of Summer Valley."

At breakfast the hot cakes with butter and honey kept them silent until after the second cup of tea.

"The woods may be a little frightening to you at first," Aunt Rose said. "There is nothing that will really harm you. When you venture out, use care about the mine holes. All about here years ago there were ore mines. They left deep holes, some since filled with water. Some are just dark pits. Some have fish in them. There used to be quite a settlement back aways in the woods, an old ore mining town named Winkler. It's been deserted for many years, although some of the buildings where the miners and their families lived are still standing. You might enjoy visiting Granny May's cabin. Granny May passed away three years ago. It's something you should see as there aren't many log cabins left."

Dressed in jeans, tennis shoes and long-sleeved shirts the girls set out to see the real log cabin. They went past the spring and the chicken house and onto a faint unused path Aunt Rose had pointed out. At the top of the hill they came to a tiny meadow and blossoming orchard.

"Ummm, smells sweet," Samme sniffed the air.

Edith stuck her nose into a cloud of blossoms and withdrew, surrendering to a half-dozen bees.

The short grass looked like a well-cared-for lawn. Pink star-shaped flowers dotted the green.

"The going is going to get tougher," Edith predicted. She was looking off to where the path led into tangled undergrowth.

The vines crowded close as if to bar the girls' entrance. Tough vines crisscrossed, leaving only a crawl space. With one last look at the pink and green carpet and a lingering sniff of blossoms the girls plunged under the vines. The pale, fruitless briars caught onto their clothes and clung.

"The forest doesn't want us to go to the deserted cabin. If it wouldn't look like I was a scared city kid, I'd go back," Samme confessed.

"I feel cold chills down my back," Edith admitted.

"You think we'll get used to it?" Samme asked.

"I hope so." Edith tried to look ahead, but she couldn't see farther than a few feet. "I've read that the woods just kind of grows on you."

"It's started to grow on me already," Samme declared, unwinding vines which encircled her ankles. . . .

"Look at all the birds in the trees. They're not afraid." Edith pointed upward to encourage her sister.

"Humph," said Samme. "Why should they be. They're safe in the trees. You and I are down on the ground where the wolves can get at us . . . bears, too."

"Wolves never come out in the daytime. At least I hope not."

"Look," Samme squealed. Edith jumped. "A baby rabbit."

A small gray rabbit sat watching them in astonishment. He flipped his ears twice and bounced away.

"No wonder that rabbit wasn't afraid of us," Edith said. "The rabbits here never see people so haven't learned to fear them. Aunt Rose said there were places in this woods people haven't set foot in for years and years."

"And I think we've found the place," Samme sighed.

"But we're going to see a real log cabin and that's that."

They pushed on, and came to a shallow creek which rippled along and around a series of stepping stones. Someone, sometime, had placed them just right for getting across—if you took long steps and a hop.

Samme untied her tennis shoes and threw them to the far side of the stream. She stood rocking back and forth, digging first her toes, then her heels into the wet, warm sand. She splashed water up over her legs.

"Look at the large bird tracks," Edith said, walking

over to the end of the sandy stretch. "Wonder if they're wild turkey tracks? Aunt Rose said there were wild turkey out this way."

A speckled water snake, turning its busy head, wound past. "A snake!" Samme squeaked.

Edith jumped and lost her balance. Plop! She landed seated in the cold water. Samme giggled. "Aunt Rose told us not to get wet."

"I know, I know." Edith went dripping to the far bank, her shoes squishing water. "Let's go. Can't be far to Granny May's cabin."

"I hope she's not there."

"Of course she's not there. She's been dead three years."

"That's what I mean." Samme shivered.

Soon a barbed wire fence overgrown with tough vines barred their way. "I'll hold the wires while you crawl through, then you hold them for me," Edith said, pulling up on the rusty wire.

The cabin stood in a grove of second-growth trees. Scattered about were small log pens. Holding hands, they approached the open door.

In the center of the cabin stood a table of rough hewn boards. Several chairs of the same design stood about near the table. One was very near and turned aside as if someone had just pushed it back. Overturned in the corner was another chair with only three legs, the missing leg beneath the table. A forlorn chest of drawers leaned against the wall. Bits of grass, twigs and dry leaves hung out of the partly opened drawers as if some animal made its home there.

Edith drew Samme around the side of the cabin. Here a very small lean-to had served as a kitchen. A rusty iron stove stood quite erect, its four iron legs propped up on blocks of wood sunk into the dirt floor. A gray, galvanized teakettle, tilted at a gentle angle rested on the front lid of the stove. Its handle stood straight up as if waiting to be picked up.

"Strange." Edith eyed the stove and the teapot.

"Creepy, staring into someone's house, even if they are . . . you know . . . passed on!"

A pair of old-fashioned women's shoes were under the stove. They might have been set there by their owner to dry.

Were they still waiting for their owner to return? Samme looked the question at Edith. As if responding one shoe began to tremble. The top widened. Two bright, bashful black eyes peered for seconds at the girls. A sensitive nose quivered and disappeared, reappeared; there was a wild dash and a brown woods rat ran outdoors.

Samme and Edith had climbed on top of the rough plank table.

"That rat had first claim rights and I was getting out of there," Samme said.

Edith climbed down and reached a hand to Samme. "We're going to have to get over jumping at the least little thing."

They looked over at a large double bed covered with an interwoven mass of woolly quilts. The colors that had once been reds and blues and yellows had been blended by time and weather into shades of gray.

"It's spooky here. Let's start back," Samme said.

"You always were a sensible girl," Edith replied.

Edith led the way in and out among the scattered log pens. They crawled under the barbed wire fence.

It was a joy to reach the friendly, tinkling creek. They sat listening to the birds and soaking up sunshine. "A crawdad," Samme said, gently pushing the shiny wet crawler with a twig. The crawdad scrambled into the mud shelter.

Edith went to look for the tiny beach with the bird tracks. She let out an unlady-like squall. "Samme, come look. The bird tracks have turned into people tracks."

The tracks were of large, bare feet, wet and fresh.

"Look."

"Friday's barefoot tracks," Samme shouted, "just like in the story of Robinson Crusoe. Let's get out of here."

4. PEOPLE TRACKS

They hurried back to Aunt Rose's.

There a blackberry pie cooled, and dinner was ready. "Set the table, girls. I'll put on the beans and corn bread and lettuce. Here are the onions." Aunt Rose put a bowl of crisp green onions in Samme's hand. "Are you ready to eat?"

"Beans and pie suit me," said Samme, and for a moment she forgot about the tracks in the sand. The sweet, warm smell of the blackberry pie filled the air. Butter melting into the hot corn bread was just right with steamy beans.

"You girls enjoy the walk to Granny May's cabin?" Aunt Rose asked. **1660471**

Edith nodded.

"I was scared," Samme admitted.

"Been a long while since I was over that way. The cabin still standing strong?"

"Looks strong, and there was a table, a stove, bed and other things in it."

Samme looked at Edith. "It was spooky, and on the way back. . . ."

Here Edith took up the story, "On the way back where you cross the creek." Aunt Rose nodded, salting her onions. "There were tracks on the sandy beach."

Aunt Rose turned her full attention to the girls. "I thought you might see turkey tracks there, I have."

"We saw turkey tracks, all right," Samme said. "And something else, too. People tracks!"

"People tracks?" Aunt Rose laid down her fork with a click.

"Yes," Edith said, "tracks of bare feet. Large, wet tracks. We hadn't heard or seen anyone when we went over. On a sandy spot at the creek we did see the turkey tracks. Then on the way back there were these footprints."

"Out of nowhere," Samme added. "We thought we were all alone, but someone must have been close by. Someone we didn't see or hear. Who in the world would be walking around in the woods barefoot? Mother said you shouldn't walk barefoot in the woods."

For seconds Aunt Rose didn't speak. She stared out the wide windows into Summer Valley. "I suppose I should have told you. I didn't want you to be afraid of walking in the woods. The tracks you saw would be those of the hermit boy."

"Hermit boy?" Edith looked at her aunt in amazement.

"I thought hermits were all old men with long beards," Samme said.

"He heard you in the forest." Aunt Rose nodded. "The cabin was his home. Granny May raised him. His name is Jason. When Granny died he was about twelve years old. People from the city came to take him away to an orphanage, thinking he would be better taken care of. Jason didn't want to go away. He had always lived in the hills, always loved the woods. So he went into hiding. Since then he has always lived in the woods."

"A wild boy." Samme gasped. "Imagine! A real wild boy."

Aunt Rose shook her head. "Not a wild boy, Samme. People in the hills think of Jason as a part of the mountains like the deer or the bobcat. Those well-meaning city folks turn up every now and then to try to find Jason and take him away. Of course they never find him, and everyone stands up and cheers."

"I wonder how he could live all alone in the woods." Samme shivered.

"Jason understands many things about the woods, such as putting the back of his hand to his mouth and sucking to make a mouse-like squeak which attracts the fox. Granny taught Jason herb lore. Sassafras makes tasty tea. Bloodroot contains a juice used as medicine by the Indians to strengthen the blood in the spring. Goldthread, a plant, can be used to cure sore throat, and aches. White Man's Foot thrives wherever a white man walks and Indian Cup grows where an Indian dies." Aunt Rose smiled. "To you city-raised girls these are just odd bits of information, but to Granny May they were the very breath of life."

"What about food?" Edith asked. "What about clothing?"

"And what about school?" Samme asked, with a touch of envy. "Doesn't he ever have to go to school?"

"Jason went to the one-room school on the main road right up to the time Granny May died. Had books at home in the cabin too in those days."

Edith and Samme were fascinated.

"Do you ever see him, Aunt Rose?"

"When Granny May was living I did. Since then I haven't actually seen Jason, but when I go berry picking or hunting mushrooms, if I turn my back my bucket fills. Then I know Jason is near. The boy has almost become a legend. He has saved many a lost calf and newborn lamb or strayed milk cow. Which is mighty near the only fortune some hill folks own. He's helped many people in sickness with herbs, dressed game for their supper, brought them wild fruit and nuts, and wood for cooking and heating. It's like having a sort of good fairy loose in the hills who goes about unseen, doing good." Aunt Rose shook her head. "One thing isn't helpful. Talk that Granny May left a safe full of money hidden. A few times we've had trouble with creepers. . . ."

"What are creepers?" Samme asked.

"I guess you'd call them sneak thieves in the city or prowlers."

"Trying to locate that lost safe?" Edith's eyes widened.

Aunt Rose nodded. "The Baron says so. I wonder if there is such a thing as a lost safe."

"Does Jason have a mother or father?" Edith asked. She scooted her chair close to Aunt Rose's, better to catch the whole story.

"Jason's father is or was an Army man. He was serving overseas at the time of Granny May's death. His mother is dead."

"Why doesn't his father come back?" Samme asked.

"That's the sad part of it, Jason's father has disappeared, the Army notified Granny May. No one's sure what happened. He may have been taken prisoner, he may be dead, or even a deserter. There's no way of knowing."

"Could there be any truth to that talk about money hidden in the safe?" Edith said. "I wonder what Jason does alone in the woods in winter."

"No one knows. Some say he lives in one of the mine pits. Some say he stays in the deep cave at the end of Summer Valley. Others say he lives in the hidden attic of the big, empty house down on the creek."

"We know that place!" Samme exclaimed. "That's as far as Henry brought us the day we came here."

"And I feel sorry for anyone who lives there," Edith added.

Aunt Rose piled the dishes. "No one really knows where he stays. The welfare people have tried to find him many times. The last time they searched the old house from attic to cellar, they found signs that someone had been there, they say! The boy is so swift, and seems to know everything that goes on; if he does stay in the old house, he could have easily slipped away." She set out the small pie plates.

"Eat your pie, girls. I don't think anyone's going to find the hermit boy until he's ready for them to find him."

"I'm not afraid of the hermit boy," Samme said. "I think he sounds nice because he was so kind to save the calves and lambs. I like him," she giggled, "and I haven't seen him yet."

"You're not likely to, either," Edith said, "especially since all those grownups couldn't find him."

"Who knows?" Aunt Rose said, smiling. "He may show himself to someone near his own age. He must get very lonely for he is only a young boy after all."

In the morning, the Baron was chopping kitchen wood for Aunt Rose while the girls watched. The crack of the axe on dry chunks ran out as clearly and regularly as the ticking of a clock. The pile of split wood grew. "You girls going to carry the wood to the house?" he asked.

"Yes, sir!"

With a sure aim the Baron halved a thick log, then sliced it into eight pieces and flung it on the pile nearby. "Help you carry, soon as I get more split. Load up like this." The Baron knelt down on the ground, stretched out his left arm full length. "Good to have long sleeves for this job." He laid the sticks of wood up his arm, one after the other. "Don't take too heavy a load." He curved his left forearm up over the sticks and placed his right arm over the top of the load. "There, that's the way."

The girls made many trips from the woodpile to the house, but they just couldn't seem to get ahead of the Baron's axe. The faster they carried, the faster he threw wood on the pile. "When the wood is all stacked by the kitchen door and the woodbox filled, we're free for the day," Edith said, puffing. With this in mind they worked harder. Finally the last chunk was split and thrown on the pile. The girls breathed a sigh of relief. Carrying wood up the hill to the house had been hard work.

Aunt Rose had been working in the field of new potatoes with Job, the mule. She came up to the spring to give the mule a drink. She was thirsty and knew he was thirsty, too.

"Tell you what," she said. "You girls can walk over with the Baron. You haven't seen that part of the woods yet. He's going over to his place to fetch Snowball, my white rabbit. The Baron took care of Snowball when I had to be away a few days."

"Good," Samme said. She had wanted to see the

Baron's house ever since Aunt Rose had told them he owned all those animals.

The girls and the Baron cut across the marsh and up the hill onto a narrow wagon road. The girls ran ahead while their companion kept a steady pace behind. The Baron was more talkative now that he knew the girls better. "See how thick the grapes are on the vines this year."

Samme looked high up. "How will you pick them?"

"The Lord means those high ones for the birds. Folks use the one that grow low along fences."

A short time later he said, "There's my place." The girls fell back, letting the Baron lead the way.

The shack, made of planed oak, blended with the woody surroundings like a wild thing. Here the Baron had his own private zoo and aviary. The entire area was hung with nesting places. There were birdhouses, gourds with tiny doorways and cans of various sizes placed high and low. There was such a flutter of winged families around each nest that the air sang. Chickens and ducks strutted underfoot in a crisscross pattern. A rangy hound dog with long-eared pups ran to greet the Baron.

"Baa! Baa! Baaaaa!"

Down from a shed roof leaped a white goat. The Baron gripped the goat's broad leather collar. "Stand close, girls. Rubin here can't abide strangers and has the meanest temper in the hills lessen he gets a jelly biscuit from their very own hands. After that he's as cuddly as a kitten." The Baron tugged the goat into the shanty. In seconds he was back, the glowering goat in one hand and two biscuits dripping jelly in the other. He gave each girl a biscuit. "Hand him the biscuit yourself. It's a change you'll see like magic in his temper."

Timidly Edith thrust the sticky biscuit at the goat's mouth. When the goat had gulped that biscuit down, Samme gave Rubin the one she held.

"Now." The Baron let loose of the leather collar. "Have to always do that with strangers or he eats them alive. Rubin here is about the best watchgoat that ever was. From now on he will treat you girls like civilized people."

Licking the last of the purple jelly off his whiskers, Rubin sidled up to the girls in turn, rubbing against them and looking lovingly into their eyes.

"From now on he's your friend for life, but heaven help anyone that meets up with Rubin that hasn't made friends by handin' out a jelly biscuit," the Baron said.

Now that the girls had made friends with Rubin they were free to look around. A half-dozen woolly sheep, two deer and a cow with a half-grown calf munched greens nearby. A squad of geese spotted the Baron and hurried up from the creek. A gander stretched out his long neck and hissed a greeting. Guinea hens called from a thicket.

The Baron used an outdoor fireplace made of fieldstone for cooking. His table and chairs were planks over large stumps. They looked as if they had grown right out of the ground.

"Only use the house for sleepin' and that in the very coldest weather." He laid dry twigs in the fireplace. "Beans and greens and butter and corn bread, that's what I favor. Your aunt keeps me in jams and jellies. Have some of those sundried apple slices whilst I put the beanpot on."

"You sure Rubin likes us now?" Samme asked.

"Stake my life on it," the Baron vowed. "Once you've handed him his jelly biscuit, he's your friend for all time." He touched a lit match to the criss-crossed twigs in the fireplace. A winding ribbon of blue smoke started upward and orange flames curled around the wood.

"Imagine the sky for a roof," Edith said.

"Never had any other roof." The Baron took an iron pot from a branch stub on a nearby tree, poured water into it and let two handfuls of white, hard beans dribble through his fist into the water. He swung the kettle over the fire.

"Just think," Samme said, marveling. "Living outside most all the year round, with a whole stream of water for your faucet, the song of birds for your stereo and—" Here Rubin let out a resounding "Baaa, baa, baa." Samme patted Rubin's now friendly head. "And a good watchgoat like Rubin."

The Baron picked up the water bucket and added water to the steaming bean kettle.

A thoughtful look crossed Edith's face as she studied the old hillman. She wondered how much he knew about the hermit boy. Only one way to find out.

The Baron set the water bucket down.

"You know the hermit boy?" Edith ventured.

"As well as any."

"You ever seen him?"

"Seen him as much as any has."

"Aunt Rose says Jason has been in the woods more than three years. Why won't he let the welfare people help him?"

"They're bound to take him away to the city, that's why!"

Samme sat down on one of the stump chairs by the table. "Aunt Rose says the hermit boy must be lonely. She thought he might be more likely to talk to someone his own age, like Edith and me."

The Baron took off his old hat and smoothed his mass of white hair. "When his Granny May was taken by the Almighty, the welfare people come for him, meanin' to do right by the boy I expect. He made hisself scarce, run off, nobody found him that day to this, nor knows where he stays."

"Not even you?"

The Baron shook his head. "By Fire, I'd take him here in a minute. I asked those welfare folk if I could take him more'n three year ago. They told me this place wasn't fitten to raise a boy, with all these critters about and no ma."

Samme's eyes flashed. "I think your, er, critters are just fine, and your fireplace and table and—and everything."

"We're going to be the hermit boy's friends," Edith said firmly, "and we *are* going to find him!"

5. TRAIL'S END

The Baron looked up. "You girls are kind to want to help Jason. Finding him will take time and . . ." The Baron looked sad. "You may be too late."

"Too late." Samme and Edith stood very still. "What do you mean?"

"I mean there's rumor going around the boy's to have Granny's cabin and the woodland that was hers

45

taken away from him 'cause of the tax due. I hear it's up to be sold in ten days. I been frettin' on it. I hear there's a heap of money due."

"That beautiful old cabin and all the forest around it," Edith cried.

Samme tightened her mouth, but her eyes sparkled. "Aunt Rose told us there's talk Granny May had a safe with money in it hidden away. Do you think it's true?"

The Baron hesitated, rubbing Rubin's snowy, soft head. "Granny May was as close-mouthed as a mink. Could be that she laid away some money. Jason's father sent her money for the boy's keep regular, and goodness knows there's no place for spending it out here. Could be Granny May had a safe, but even if she did, where is it? It's just gone."

"If we only knew where Jason's father was." Edith frowned.

The Baron scooped up Snowball, the white rabbit. "There's those that say he's an Army deserter. There are those that say he was captured and being held prisoner. As well as we can understand, the Army don't know for sure."

"The only sure thing," Edith sighed. "Is that he isn't here to help."

Rubin rubbed against the three of them. "Gives a body a puzzle to think on."

As they arrived at the house, Aunt Rose finished her daily garden work and set the water on for tea.

"Just in time." Aunt Rose called as they came up the path. She took Snowball from Samme and placed him on the floor. The cats watched jealously through the door. Snowball hopped off to look about behind the iron stove.

Aunt Rose put a coffeecake on the table and fresh fruit. "I rode the mule to the mailbox. Here is the paper."

Taking the newspaper, Edith spread the pages out on the table. Sipping milk, she began to read. "Oh," she breathed, her eyes darkening. "Look, Aunt Rose. Samme, see what I've found." The three of them bent over the printed page, all eyes following Edith's finger down the column. "See, the land and cabin thereon to be sold for taxes. Jason May's land. In ten days. The Baron was right."

Aunt Rose pressed her hand to her lips. "Seven hundred and fifty dollars. That is a lot of money. We can't let this happen. We won't let Jason lose his land."

Edith folded the paper. "Samme and I must find Jason. Get a message to him about the sale. It's possible he may have the money that Granny May was said to have in the safe."

Aunt Rose nodded. "If Jason is found and should he have the money to pay the taxes, there is still a problem. How do we keep the law from taking Jason away from the land he knows and loves so well?"

The meal was finished in deep thoughtful silence.

After the dishes were washed and put away the afternoon passed uneventfully. Edith and Samme talked in bed.

"Wonder how we should go about finding Jason,"

Edith said. "To do any real good we will also have to find the safe. If there is a safe . . . and if there is money in it."

Samme took a deep breath. "If the hill people can't find Jason, and the welfare people can't find Jason and even the Baron says he doesn't know where he is . . . we are going to have to look hard to find him and the money . . . in ten days."

"How could the city welfare people find anything in that woods?" Edith said.

"And the hill folks don't want to find Jason for they feel sure he'll be taken away if he's found. Yet look at it their way. Does it seem right to let a homeless boy live alone in the woods year-after-year like a deer or a rabbit?"

"That's the way the welfare people see it. What if Jason broke his leg? Yes, the people from the city feel they are doing the right thing."

"Do you," Samme asked, "feel that they are doing the right thing by always trying to catch Jason and take him away from the hills?"

"I'm not sure," Edith answered thoughtfully. "The hill folks are on one side, the city folks are on the other side and Jason is somewhere in the middle, yet neither side knows where the middle is."

All of a sudden a low sound came through the window. Someone was singing. The girls remained still, listening. Aunt Rose had heard it, too. She had gotten out of bed and was standing in the doorway of the cabin. The girls ran to her.

The notes of the song gathered strength and flew

towards them. They stood and listened, looking upward into the woods.

"It's him. It's Jason, isn't it?" Somehow Samme knew it had to be. Aunt Rose nodded, her eyes sad. "Sometimes he sings. Many folks have heard him. It's an old song he learned from Granny May. He can't be very far away."

The rippling notes rose and fell in a fine, clear melody, and then the singing came to an end. The night insects and treefrogs began their own shrill song, but the human voice and the boy singer were gone.

"Let's run into the woods and try to see him!" Samme cried, catching Edith's hand and pulling her up.

"It's no use," Aunt Rose said with a catch in her voice. "Rest easy. The boy has seen you and Edith about. The song is for you. Now he's gone . . . wherever he goes at night."

It was just after daylight when the girls awoke the next morning. They dressed quickly. "Come on," Edith said, going to the kitchen cupboard. "I know what we can do. Let's leave some corn bread and honey for the hermit boy. We'll take it into the woods and put it in some handy place about where the singing came from."

Samme hurried to the tall cupboard for a small jar to put the honey in. She filled the jar and put the lid on tight. "That's to keep the ants from getting it before the hermit boy does."

Edith cut and wrapped the firm, yellow corn bread.

They put the corn bread and honey on a thick, flowered platter, climbed the hill and paused at the edge of the woods. There was no sound, so on into the trees they went until they found a smooth-topped stump. It was just like a small table. Here they placed the platter; they stood a minute as if hoping the hermit boy might appear, then they started back to the house. Several times turning to look, but only the quivering leaves stirred.

After lunch they went up the hill, through the long golden sunbeams of the afternoon, and into the shadowed trees. Without words each was asking, did he come or didn't he come to eat the food they had placed on the stump!

Here was the platter. Clean. Not a crumb on it. The wax paper the corn bread had been wrapped in was folded in a neat square.

"As clean as if the cats had followed us up here and licked it," Edith said.

"Cats don't eat honey," Samme said, jumping up and down. "He ate it. He ate it." She ran round and round the stump. "Cats don't fold wax paper into neat squares."

"I think he did eat it," Edith said. "But how can we be sure?"

"Simple," Samme said. "We'll just look for footprints. Barefoot prints."

The longer they looked for footprints, the more positive they became that no one had eaten the corn bread. Because there were no footprints to be found.

"Ghosts ate it!" Samme cried. "There are no tracks and ghosts don't leave tracks so. . . ."

"No such thing," Edith said firmly. "It's just that tracks can't show up on leaves and moss. You and I walked all around here and do you see any of our prints?"

"Anyway, the honey and corn bread are gone and I think Jason had it for lunch."

"We better go back to the house," Edith said. She picked up the platter. "We have chores to do. Hey look!"

There, where the platter had set, was printed J. M. in large black letters.

"It's him," Samme shouted. "Let's go find him. Let's go. J.M. That stands for Jason May."

"We won't start off just like this," Edith said soberly. She stared at the black letters. This was the second contact with the boy of the woods. The song . . . and these letters in print.

"We'll have to think this out, lay a plan."

"Work out a plan so he'll come to us!" Samme cried. "I have a great idea. By Fire," she said with a giggle, using the Baron's favorite expression, "fry a big platter of chicken and walk around in the woods with it steaming. That should bring him to us."

Edith clamped her hand to her forehead. "You dreamer! When others have been looking for the hermit boy for three years. How could we find him in one day, even with a powerful weapon like fried chicken? But let's try it anyway and tomorrow we'll pack a lunch and walk over to the old mining town Aunt Rose told us about. He might be living in one of those old houses." Then touching the letters with her fingertips, Edith noticed that the black came off on her hand.

"He printed these initials with burned wood." She rubbed the printed letters until they blended into the wood and disappeared. "No one must know yet. It might bring searchers into the woods."

They went back to the house, carrying the empty platter and the little honey jar.

By the time the chores were done it was late afternoon. Edith brought a bucket of hickory nuts from the loft over the little black-and-white pig's pen. They were going to crack the nuts, pick out the good inside and make hickory nut cookies.

"Get the hammer and come out," Edith called inside to Samme. It had been Samme's job to polish the black enameled table. Getting no reply, Edith poked her nose in the kitchen door. The table top was gleaming. Edith went into the bedroom. She went to the bedroom door and looked outside. There sat Samme under the squirrel tree. She was almost out of sight under a pile of rags. She was absorbed in tearing the rags apart, into strips about four inches long.

Edith stared down at the whole business. "What on earth are you doing? Starting your own rag factory?"

Samme looked up, blinking as if waking from a dream. "Help me sack these up. These rag strips are going to keep us from getting lost when we go into the woods to hunt Jason." She held a strip up, dangling it. "When we get into the woods, we'll just tie these to a twig every so often, then when we're ready to return home, all we have to do is follow the strips."

"That's the silliest idea I ever heard of!"

"You have a better one?"

"Well-l-l, no."

"Okay, then let's sack them."

So they filled two large plastic bags with the strips and shoved them under the bed. "Our plan to find the hermit boy of Summer Valley has begun," Samme announced.

"Then let's start to crack and pick those nuts so we can make cookies. We need plenty of food for the trip tomorrow."

It was still dark the next morning when a voice calling in the kitchen fetched Aunt Rose out of bed and awoke the girls. Aunt Rose dressed in a hurry. "Have to go over the ridge," she called out. "Family needs me." The door slammed.

Samme rolled over. "We're orphans."

"No, we're free. Free for the whole day to go into the woods and find the hermit boy, or have him find us." Without the cheer of sunlight Samme took a dim view of the plan. "What if we get so lost that no one ever finds us?"

"What about your rags we were to tie on twigs?"

Samme snorted. "I can just see the headlines now:

'Hermit Boy Found by Girls with Bag of Rags'."

"Come on, get dressed."

Samme began to come awake. They hurried, preparing for their adventure in the woods.

Edith sped here and there. "Gather things up neatly. We'll be tired when we return. Pack the cookies and the biscuits together."

"Let's not forget the bucket of fried chicken," Samme sang out. "We won't have to carry water. There seem to be springs of good water everywhere."

Edith rattled around in the cupboard. "I've found some matches, so we can build a fire. We can heat water for tea and heat the chicken if we want to, as long as we're careful with the fire."

"And bake potatoes," Samme chimed in. "Always carry a rope when you walk in the woods, too. The Baron said so. We'll take the rope from the peg at the barn as we pass."

"A thin blanket, too. It'll be easy to carry. We can put everything except the chicken in the canvas bag with the straps. And we'd better leave a note. Aunt Rose said always leave a note on the table when we went away from the house."

"Okay," Samme slipped a piece of paper from the cupboard drawer. Edith printed the message in large block letters:

GONE TO THE WOODS
TO FIND YOU KNOW WHO

"Think she'll know who?" Samme asked.

"Just how many people are lost in the woods?"

"One now," Samme grinned. "By evening there may be three."

The crowd of cats followed the girls to the spring, which was midway between the house and the barn. The girls stopped to pour milk for them before going on.

"Shall I take a cat?" Samme asked. "If we get lost, maybe the cat would lead us home."

"The cat would just be lost, too." Edith started up the hill. "Let's get the rope."

Pulling the rope from the peg, Samme wound it around and around her waist.

They paused a minute to look at the corn bread and honey stump.

The girls started down a faint lane made long ago by heavy wagons, carrying ore from the mines. Aunt Rose had told them it lead to the old mining town.

"We're headed for a ghost town!" Samme said.

"Not a ghost town," Edith said. "That's just an expression people use. Where we're going is just a bunch of broken-down houses that people used to live in."

"Humph," Samme said, frowning. "I don't think I'm going to like that place any more than I would like a ghost town."

"You want to find Jason, don't you?"

"'Course I do." Samme slogged along grimly in the early morning damp grass. "And so do you."

They tramped down the rough lane, climbing over fallen logs, jumping over deep ruts. Soon both sides of the trail looked the same. The branches of tall trees met overhead in a green ceiling. Flashes of yellow sunlight lay in golden patches on the forest floor.

"Isn't this lovely?" Edith said. "I can see why the hermit boy wanted to stay here always."

Samme looked around. "No dime stores here, but the air and sun feel good. I could go on walking and never stop."

"Don't try it," Edith warned. "It's time we had a rest."

She scrambled over a bank to a ledge of white rock just above a narrow stream.

Samme followed, looking around with care. "I like to see what's around before I sit down. Hey, look!"

A turtle with a yellow shell scrambled under the ledge. Pulling off their tennis shoes, the girls swished their bare feet back and forth quickly in the icy water. Startled minnows fled north, south, east and west.

Samme drew her wet feet up, making bare prints on the warm rocks. "How far you think it is to the old town?"

Edith looked up the bank toward the trail they had been following. "Can't tell. Not far now, I guess."

"Good grief," Samme wailed. "You know what we did. We forgot the rag strips."

"Don't worry. Put on your shoes, let's get going."

Samme tried to make the rope wound around her waist more comfortable. "At least with this food, even if we get lost, we won't starve to death for a day or two."

They walked on, over rotten logs, around briar patches. "Wonder if there's an extra room for lost people in that place Jason stays," Samme muttered as the woods grew wilder and wilder. Suddenly Edith stopped.

"We've come to the end."

"Ours?"

"The trail's end. There's nothing here. No more trail. No more nothing." Samme hurried to her sister's side. "We're on the edge of a cliff. What do we do now?"

6. OVER THE CLIFF

The girls looked down into the tops of the trees, thinking. Samme clung to a stout grapevine. "Looking down into the tops of trees should make me feel like a giant;

instead it makes me feel small, small, small. Besides, I'm allergic to high places."

"Then," Edith said, "you have acrophobia. A morbid fear of high places."

"Yes! My feelings to a T. I suggest we go around instead of down."

"There isn't any around. I know. Let's tie the rope to both of us, the way mountain climbers do and climb down. I'm sure we can manage."

Samme snorted, but she consented to having the rope tied around her waist.

"There," Edith said, tightening the last knot. "Slip that bucket of fried chicken on your arm so you can have both hands free. Hold onto every stout root and branch on the way down. Find every secure foothold you can. Here goes!"

Edith slid over the side, feet first. Pebbles and assorted rocks slid with her, rolling out of sight.

Samme held onto her grapevine with an iron grip. When Edith stopped sliding, she took hold of a stunted tree while Samme scrambled in a cloud of dust and pebbles down beside her and kept on going down a ways, then stopped. Then it was Edith's turn to pass Samme. This was repeated several times. The girls' jeans were the color of red clay.

"See anything yet?" Samme called down to Edith.

"I see the roofs of buildings," Edith shouted. "It's the old town, all right. The building just below looks as if it were the main one. The main office perhaps."

Edith was sitting on a narrow ledge, her legs dangling. "Come this far."

Samme lowered herself to join her sister. Dirt, leaves, and small stones tumbled on every side. "Oh," she said, her eyes widening. "That's an eerie-looking set of buildings." She looked down onto the roofs blended into a wild growth of trees and brush. "You really think the hermit boy lives there?" Edith said.

"Let's go down." Samme tried to guess the distance to solid ground. The roof of the largest building was just below.

"Let's not jump down on the rooftop, the wood might be rotted." Edith scooted over. Samme followed along the ledge.

They inched their way over the ledge and down a few feet until it seemed safe to jump. They landed with a thump and stood up.

"What bothers me," Samme said, "is . . . how are we going to get back up, to go home?"

"First things first." Edith took her sister's hand, helping her through the thick grass. Flowers sprinkled the tangled growth with color . . . Iris and lemon lilies, lilac thickets and thorny rosebushes grew lushly between the gray houses.

Each house leaned on its neighbor in a tired, familiar manner. A few had given up and lay in heaps on the ground.

The girls entered the long narrow building which was just under the cliff; a swift scramble of dainty feet indicated four-footed householders.

"Rat ranch," Samme said, drawing back.

"This had to be the office," Edith said. "There's the desk."

Yellowed papers fluttered as the floor vibrated with each step. The girls backed out into the sunlight. Exploring the town, they tramped through overgrown yards and over slanting doorsteps. The forlorn houses seemed to watch them with window eyes. At the end of a row of broken buildings a lively spring bubbled off into a minnow-filled creek. Here they found a rough stone bench, a fireplace of fieldstone, a dented brass boiler and a cracked tin scrub board. This spot must have been the old town's washing and watering spot.

Bright yellow finches flashed in brown cattails. Rainbow-colored dragonflies zipped over the water. The town had been dead for 50 years yet the area of the spring bubbled with life. They saw two striped chipmunks, sitting on a red cedar stump.

"Guess it's been a long time since anyone's had lunch here," Edith said. "Except maybe the hermit boy." She sat down on the stone bench.

Samme flipped open the thin blanket and made it into a large, flowing square with a snap of her wrists. "This will be our tablecloth."

Edith gathered small twigs. "This fireplace is perfect for heating water to make tea." She laid the dry sticks crisscross fashion in the fireplace, then touched them with a lighted match.

Samme pulled a tin pan and two cups from the pack. She filled the pan with water and placed it on the fire.

Taking up the bucket of chicken, she placed it within easy reach.

Edith added pinches of crisp tea leaves to the warming water in the pan. She watched as the dark bits swirled, settled to the bottom and rose again in silver bubbles as the water heated.

"After we use our blanket for a tablecloth, you know what we are going to use it for?" Samme asked.

Edith shook her head.

"A bed, that's what, I need a nap. Close your eyes," Samme said as they were eating. "Imagine it's fifty years ago. Don't you see the powerful mules pulling loads of iron ore?"

Edith played along. "I see a huffing, puffing engine on the railroad tracks. The rails aren't rusted. The ties aren't rotted. Everything is new and shiny. Flat cars are being loaded. Men and boys carrying tools are running back and forth!"

"Hear the train whistle." Samme put her hand behind her ear. "The train's pouring out smoke and steam. Children are wading in the stream. See, there's a small girl playing in the sand." She jumped up. "Shall we explore a few of those old houses? Perhaps Jason lives in one of them?"

"None of them are fit to live in," Edith said. But she stood up.

The girls ploughed into the tall grass, crushing a path to a gaping, vine-strangled doorway of a long, narrow building.

The building had been a bunkhouse. Rows of narrow wooden bunks, some still covered with straw mattresses, lined the walls on two sides.

A monstrous full-bellied, wood-burning stove stood guard at the far wall, looking as if it were good for another thousand years, even if the stovepipe hung dangling.

Small animals skittered!

"Ugh! I don't like the looks of this," Samme said. She stepped high over some broken crockery on the floor. Moldering rags and dented cooking ware lay scattered about.

They returned to the friendly spring. A fat ground hog, looking like a well-fed householder, gazed unworried from a broken step.

Samme shook the blanket into a bed. The girls lay down and were soon asleep.

Samme awoke first, blinking. She shook Edith.

"Good grief!" Edith jumped up. "We slept longer than we should have. Let's get packed." She began to gather up the teacups and water pan. "Get the bucket of chicken. Wrap the rope around your waist. . . ."

"Tug that barge. Tote that bale," Samme sang, moving fast.

Edith threw her the circle of rope. "Let's go," she said.

"Where? We could go north, south, east or west. But the way we need to go to get home is straight up."

Looking toward the towering height of the cliff, the girls knew that although they had made it down they could never climb up.

"We must go east. This town's west of Aunt Rose's house."

"You mean," Samme asked, "if we go east far enough, and long enough, we'll find the house? Which way is east?"

"Look at the sun. The sun goes down in the west. We'll go in the opposite direction."

"We better go in the opposite direction soon. The sun's about to set."

It was true. The old buildings of the town were sunk in the deep shade of late evening. Only the fireplace and the white stone bench held a glow of sunlight. A few steps away black shadows lay, moving closer each moment. The evening air was damp and cool.

"We may have to spend the night in the woods," Edith said quietly.

Samme turned toward her sister, thinking she had misunderstood. Edith was staring across the roof of the broken building at the face of the cliff. Samme's gaze followed her sister's. On the very ledge where they had stood, a lean gray form, like a dog, only larger than the average dog, sat back on its haunches. It turned its long head from side to side, then looked up into the darkening sky and let out a long, eerie howl. The frightening sound rose and fell, lasting for minutes. The girls stood spellbound. The animal rose, looked around once, sniffed the air and moved off, blending into moss-covered rocks.

"A wolf!"

Samme shivered. "Let's get out of here. If I have to

sleep in the woods tonight, I don't want it to be in this spot."

"Let's go over to the railroad track and follow that. Railroad tracks always lead somewhere!"

"Even fifty-year-old tracks?" Samme sighed. "If we had only remembered the bag of rags."

"Rags or no rags, we couldn't climb up that cliff."

The girls tramped over the rough uneven ground to the railroad. Samme kicked at the rusty rails and decayed wooden ties. There was an explosion in the grass nearby and a startled family of quail burst into the open.

Edith jumped. "Good grief! What was that?" Then she saw the family of fat, brown birds seeking a new spot for the night, and relaxed.

Samme began prying the lid off the chicken bucket. "Save the rest of the chicken," Edith said. "We'll need it for breakfast."

"I'm not going to eat it," Samme replied, prying all the harder. "I'm just taking the lid off so that the hermit boy can smell the fried chicken. He'll come for the chicken, then I'll ask him to take us home."

"If it were only that simple. But go ahead . . . try anything. Take off the lid."

So they sat there in the deepening twilight, with the lid off the chicken bucket and waited, and waited, and waited.

Finally Edith stood up. "This is the silliest thing we've done yet. Put the lid on that bucket this minute. I'm getting so hungry smelling that chicken myself that I may fall upon it and eat it all up."

"Me, too." Samme clamped the lid back on the bucket. Then she raised her head, listening.

"What was that sound?"

Edith looked troubled. "Sounded like thunder to me." She put her hand out, palm up. A drop of water splashed.

A streak of lightning flicked off the cliff. Thunder rumbled. Black clouds rolled and tumbled one over the other.

The girls ran back toward the frail buildings of the old town. The long office building seemed to offer the best shelter, and they headed for it. Before they could reach it, they were soaking wet. Water ran from their hair, down over their foreheads off their noses.

Edith pushed Samme through the paper-strewn doorway as a smashing thunderbolt shook the ground underfoot.

The building shuddered like an animal, cringing under the torrent of water. The walls swayed, threatening to collapse.

Edith set her pack down. "Have to make the best of it," she said.

"Right now there isn't any best!" Samme said, untying the heavy rope from her waist.

The rain hung in silver, splashing curtains at the broken door and windows. Flashing lightning revealed even the darkest cobweb-filled corners.

"Look," Samme said, pointing. "On the wall. Pairs of old-fashioned bib overalls. Dry!" She unsnagged a pair from a nail. "I'm putting these on."

"Those are men's overalls. Too large for you," Edith said.

"So? I wasn't planning a style show!" Samme struggled out of her soaked jeans and shirt. She shook the ancient overalls. "Out spiders! Out spiders!" She shook the overalls until the cloth snapped. Then she stuck her legs into the flapping opening and buckled the broad shoulder straps. She rolled up the extra length around her ankles.

The sight of Samme in the baggy clothes was too much for Edith. Pointing, she began to laugh. "Hand me a pair."

It was Samme's turn to laugh. "Let's look into the pockets," she said.

"We might draw out a handful of little pink mice!" Edith answered.

"A handful of baby mice wouldn't bother me a bit with all the problems we already have. Come on." Samme shoved her own hand deep into the sack-like pocket. She pulled out a yellowed cloth sack half-full of tobacco. The other hand came out with two pennies in it. Edith fished out a large red handkerchief, several pebbles and a broken pocketknife.

"My man didn't smoke. He was healthier than your man," Edith said.

"Maybe so, but my man had money and yours was broke." Samme laughed.

"I feel a little better," Edith admitted.

Samme looked from the storm outside to the thickening shadows lurking on all sides. "If we stay in here tonight I am going to sleep close to the door for a quick getaway."

"This building is the strongest of the lot. At least we're out of the wind and rain."

"I'll pull a drawer out of this desk and we can use it for a seat," Samme said, giving the top drawer a mighty tug.

CRASH!

Samme and the drawer hit the floor together. The ends, sides and bottom of the drawer flew in different directions.

Stub pencils and rusty paper clips shot into the air.

Samme, from her nest of paper clips, groaned.

Edith stooped to help her up.

"Say! The rain has stopped," Samme said. She bounded out the door.

"Wait! Wait for me," Edith called.

Samme rounded the corner. The next thing Edith heard was a sickening crash. She ran after Samme.

Samme had run over a covering of decayed boards and vanished into a pit.

Dark water with bits of wood and wiggling things washed over her. Gasping, Samme tread water in the darkness.

Edith lay down, reaching as far into the opening as she dared. There was no time for terror, even if her blood ran as cold as the water in the pit. She pulled the stoutest board from the pile that lay near and, as

Samme's second frightened cry reached her ears, tilted the board down toward her sister.

"Keep afloat with this. I'll run back for the rope." Edith bounded around the corner of the long building.

The faster Edith tried to run, the more she slipped in the red, sticky clay mud. A nightmare. Praying, she ran over the rotted doorsill and snatched up the coil of heavy rope.

7. SAVED

Clutching the lowered board, Samme kicked her feet. The water was freezing cold. She looked up from the dark hole, waiting, praying.

Then it came, a strong rope with a loop tied in the end. Samme caught the loop, slipped it first over one shoulder, then the other. Sure hands began to pull her upward. She braced her feet against the muddy walls. Oh, blessed relief, she was at the top. She scrambled over the edge and fell cold and trembling on the grass.

Just then, Edith hurried around the corner with the rope in her hands. Seeing Samme safe, she stood stunned for one second, then she ran to her sister's side.

"You're out. Thank goodness. How did you do it alone?"

"Alone! I didn't do it alone. You lowered the rope. The rope with the loop on the end. I put it over my shoulders and you . . . you pulled me out."

Edith drew Samme away from the edge of the treacherous pit. She stared at the still coiled rope in her own hand. The rope she hadn't needed. They both looked at a second rope that lay close by. That rope had a loop in the end.

Edith gasped. "I—I just got here."

Samme picked up the second rope. She began rolling it into a neat coil. Her hands were shaking.

"It had to be Jason who helped you out," Edith said softly. "Now Jason has rescued something besides new calves and lambs."

Darkness had set in now. The complete darkness that comes on a moonless night. The girls went back to the office building, gathered their belongings by feeling, went back outside, and sat close together against a wall. Two dark blotches. They talked, trying not to notice how wet and chilled they were.

Then out of the blanket of night a rod of light appeared. It was small at first, then, drawing closer, it became larger. A length of light, the color of which the girls had never seen before. A voice, the master of the light, spoke:

"Follow me, I will lead you home." The voice belonged to a boy, a very young man. The hermit boy.

Like actors in a silent film, the girls followed the voice and the light. What was this glow with a greenish color? Not a lantern. Certainly not a flashlight. For while it was easily seen, it made no real light. The girls stayed as close as possible to the tall shape ahead.

It occurred to Edith what the glow must be. "Fox fire," she whispered. "I've read about it. It's found in the decaying wood of logs or stumps. It can't be seen in the daylight but it gives off a firefly-like light at night."

At the low-voiced bid of their guide, the girls rested. "I just don't think I can get up again," Samme declared as she slumped down on some thickly matted leaves. She wondered if she had ever been so tired. When the voice told them to start walking again, the thought of the soft, dry bed at home helped her to her feet. Edith urged her gently along. The green-white glow rose and fell as they moved forward.

It seemed as if they walked for hours in silence, at last the outline of the log barn appeared against the sky, touched by the pale light of a late-rising quarter moon. The girls turned to thank their guide, but he was gone. Only the green glow from a piece of fox fire which had fallen to the ground marked the spot.

It was as if the walk through the night had been a dream. Edith picked the chip up between her fingertips. A diamond of the forest which lived and sparkled by night, only to turn into decayed wood with the dawn. Samme touched it to be sure it was real. Edith folded her fingers over the strange piece of wood.

"Aunt Rose has the lamp lit," Samme said. "She must be awake."

"Some of the neighbors are here, too," Edith said, as a small group of people carrying a lantern came down the path to meet them.

Aunt Rose put her arms around the girls. "You did give us a fright. I went to the neighbors to ask about you. They've come back with me—and the Baron, too."

"By Fire." The Baron took off his hat in a gesture of profound relief. "We all just knew Jason would get you girls home in good shape."

The smiling neighbors pressed forward to greet the girls. "Us hill folks have learned to count on the hermit boy of Summer Valley. You girls must be very tired."

"Guess we all better settle down and get some rest." Aunt Rose thanked the kindly neighbors and said goodnight. The girls were no sooner in bed than sound asleep.

Down at the spring the next morning, later than usual, the girls were doing the washing. Samme was hanging the freshly washed clothes of the day before on the wire line. She looked over at Edith, who was stuff-

ing the large overalls they'd found in the old town into
the fire. The smell of burning cloth filled the air.
Smoke billowed and sparks flew as Edith pushed the
last remnants of the muddy, damp material onto the
hot woodcoals. For a moment Samme closed her eyes
and tried not to think again of the dark and slimy
sinkhole and her struggle to escape. There was the
rope over by the spring that the hermit boy had lowered to her. She was thankful again that he had been
near when they had needed him so much. This afternoon they would try to return it to him.

The washing done, they filled the tub again. They
bathed and washed their hair, then sat beside the
spring and let the sun dry it.

Now they, like other people of the hills, owed a debt
to Jason. The boy who was always near when needed
but never seen. The boy whose home—what there was
of it—was to be taken away so soon. More than likely
he did not even know about the approaching sale of his
cabin and land. In a foolish flush of vanity the girls
were sorry they'd been caught wearing baggy overalls.

Samme reached into the pocket of her fresh jeans.
"If it weren't for the two pennies I found in the pocket
of those overalls, I could hardly believe it happened."
She held the two pennies in her open palm.

"And this," Edith said, opening her hand. She dis-
played a small piece of decayed wood. "The fox fire."

"Looks like any other piece of wood in the daytime,"
Samme said, studying the chip. "See the dates on these
pennies, nineteen nine and nineteen eleven. They're

old. Wonder if they're worth anything." Closing her hand and shoving the coins back into her pocket, Samme said sadly, "Even if they were worth a hundred dollars, it wouldn't be enough to save the cabin and the land for Jason."

"Come on," Edith said, hoping to cheer her sister up with action. "Everything is finished here. Let's go over to Granny May's cabin."

"Edith, do you think Jason knows the cabin is going to be sold?"

"I don't suppose he does. We'll write him a note about it. Let's hurry, we'll make up some peanut butter sandwiches."

"Mustn't forget to leave a note for Aunt Rose and we can write the note for Jason now, too."

Samme took a sheet of clean paper from the cupboard as Edith wrapped the sandwiches.

"Shall I start, 'Jason . . . or Dear Jason'?"

"I think Dear Jason would be quite all right." Edith reached for the pencil, but Samme held onto it.

"He pulled me out of the sinkhole. Let me start the note." In large, clear letters she began, DEAR JASON . . . and stopped at a loss. "You take over," she said, pushing the paper to Edith. Edith wrote under Samme's DEAR JASON:

WE WANTED YOU TO KNOW THAT GRANNY MAY'S CABIN IS TO BE SOLD. MONEY IS NEEDED TO SAVE THE CABIN AND THE LAND. TO PAY THE TAXBILL. WE WANT TO HELP YOU.

"How's that?" Edith asked.

Samme nodded. Edith put the peanut butter sand-wiches in a bag, and handed it to Samme. She took up the broom and dustpan as they went out the door.

"What are those for?" Samme asked.

"An idea just came to me. Let's clean the cabin."

The narrow, brushy path to Granny May's cabin was familiar ground to the girls now. Each briar and cling-ing vine was pushed impatiently out of the way. The girls had a job to do and a few thorns were not going to stand in the way. They crawled under the barbed wire fence and hurried between the small second-growth trees and the scattered pens and little sheds. What was that sound?

"Voices!"

Edith touched Samme's shoulder as a sign of cau-tion. Could it be their friend, the hermit boy? No, there were several different voices. The girls knelt out of sight behind one of the low pens, and peeked be-tween the wide cracks.

Three people came around the end of the cabin. The first was a heavy, round-shouldered man, with a half-bald head and a round face. He was doing most of the talking, gesturing with one hand and at times fan-ning himself with a large straw hat which he carried in the other hand. Prepared for the rough country, he wore leather boots and a long-sleeved, checkered shirt.

A man and woman followed him. Townspeople by the looks of them. The woman kept watching around her feet as she minced along the ground in skimpy white sandals. The man wore polished black shoes and looked out of place in a suit and tie.

"Make a first-class summer place," the half-bald man said. "People like yourselves are just grabbing up these out-of-the-way places."

The girls hadn't planned to eavesdrop, just stay out of sight, but they couldn't help it. It sounded as if the round-shouldered man were trying to sell the cabin.

The girls were sure this was so when he pointed out how quiet and peaceful a home here would be. How it wouldn't take much to tear down the old cabin. Samme's face turned red with anger when he said that. The girls watched as the three adults disappeared from sight into the wooded area above the cabin. A few minutes later they returned, puffing. The salesman pointed to the length of Summer Valley which could be seen from the cabin, then they went down to the spring. A sure selling point with city folks.

"Let's stay out of sight a few minutes more," Edith whispered. "See what else he's up to."

"A crook. I say he's a crook," Samme whispered back.

"Hasn't the decency to wait for the tax sale," Edith said. "He's so sure there's no one to pay the debt. So sure he'll get the cabin and the land at the sale. He's already lining up a buyer."

"Greed," Samme announced as she moved for a better view.

"Makes me so mad. If we just knew where Jason's father was, he would help."

"If the whole U.S. Army isn't able to find Jason's father, it's sure we can't."

Full of gloom the girls watched as the town couple

dipped their hands into the cold water of Jason's spring. They pulled them out quickly, gasping in approval at the coldness of the water. The salesman nodded as if he had proved a point.

The girls were about to leave their hiding place when a young man appeared at the cabin door. Jason. It had to be. Their first good look at the hermit boy of Summer Valley. The boy was slim, young, alert. His hair was as thick and black as Samme's. His far-seeing eyes were gray and his lips parted slightly as he looked at the disappearing trio. Then he moved out of sight inside the cabin.

Samme bounded up. She was determined to talk to the hermit boy. Edith ran after her to the cabin. She wished there could have been a more civilized way to meet the hermit boy again than running him down pell-mell. She followed Samme into the cabin. It was empty!

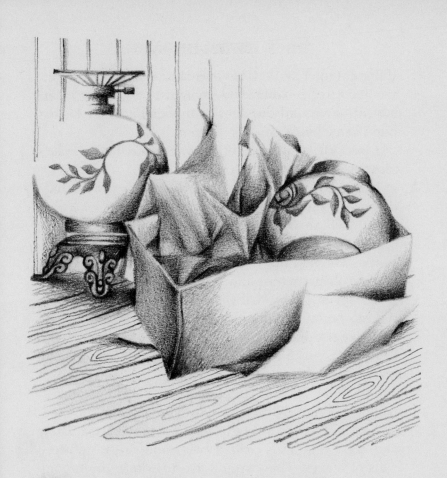

8. INTO THIN AIR

Crickets skittered, disturbed by the giant intruders. Edith tested a chair for sitting purposes. She rocked it first on the back legs, then on the front legs to be sure it would hold her weight. She sat down.

"He disappeared into thin air." Samme leaned against the table.

"He couldn't do that. No one can."

"Where is he—where did he vanish? I could see the only windows and the door to the kitchen lean-to. He didn't leave by those."

"I just don't know," Edith answered. "Unless he has a secret hideaway."

"When he's ready, we'll see him. I feel sure of that. Meanwhile there are things to do."

"Like what?" Samme asked sourly.

Edith went back to the shed, getting the broom and dustpan she had left behind in the excitement. "We're going to clean up the cabin."

"Where and how shall we start?"

"Let's begin by taking these rags off the floor. Then we'll take the old quilts from the bed and air them."

Gingerly picking up the rags, the girls piled them beyond the cabin yard out of sight.

"The floor is in better shape than I imagined," Edith observed. "Now that we can see it." She stamped her feet to test the strength of the wide boards. They were solid. The girls carried twigs and swept up armloads of leaves. They were down to where the broom could be used.

"Let's make the bed." Both girls eyed the heaped, moldly blankets. It took some courage. Samme thought she could see the faint outline of Granny May still lying there, for the lumped quilts held a strangely human shape. She pushed the idea from her mind and laid hold of the top cover.

"If Jason is watching us," Samme said, "I hope he'll understand we're only trying to clean up his cabin."

"Wonder what that salesman will think when he comes back and finds it changed."

"Maybe he'll think it's Granny May's ghost at work," Samme muttered, a bit pale at the thought.

"On with the job." Edith took hold of the next layer of bedding.

A loose, colorless nightgown, its long sleeves waving in the gentle afternoon breeze, fluttered to the floor.

Edith picked up the garment by the shoulders. The material was flannel, woven in a faint stripe. The empty thing hung meekly.

"I'm grateful for one thing," Samme said. "That we're doing this job in the bright light of day."

Edith laughed to conceal the eerie sensation which seemed to flow from the limp gown into her very fingertips. She scooped up several long gray underslips, threw them over her arm along with the nightgown and strung them over low-hanging bushes in the yard.

Three more quilts were pulled from the bed and taken outside. Two pair of ancient black stockings were found under the stale feather pillows. With straining and heaving the girls pulled the ungainly feather-filled mattress from the bed and carried it out the door.

At last they were down to the framework of the bed. It was an old, old bed with iron rails and supports. The rails were held to the bedstead by round iron pins half an inch thick. Rust lay in red chips on the floor below —and something else. A box of yellowed, stained cardboard, just waiting to be looked into. What passed for bedsprings was heavy rope woven back and forth between the rails.

"Get a rock," Edith said. "We'll pound these iron pins loose. Then we can take the bed apart, haul the pieces down to the spring, and wash them."

Samme went out the door, then hurried back with a heavy rock. It took some lusty pounding before the pins gave way and fell with a thud on the floor. It took minutes of pushing and pulling to get the head and foot of the bed and the rope frame out the door. Samme collapsed in the doorway to catch her breath.

"This is the first time I've ever played house for real. It's hard work."

"What would you guess is in this box?" Edith asked, touching the dusty cardboard with her toe.

"I can't guess," Samme sighed, "and I haven't the courage to look because if the box isn't full of money, it won't help us a bit. Besides I'm bushed!"

"Girls! Girls!" It was Aunt Rose calling. She was making her way between the log chicken pens. Good thing they had left a message about going to the cabin.

Aunt Rose stood, one foot ahead of the other in midstride, looking at the quilts airing and the gown and underslips waving from the bushes. The girls waited for her reaction. They had not stopped to think how this cleaning up of Granny May's cabin might appear to a grownup.

Aunt Rose walked over to them. "Odd how the cabin should be littered all this time and no one thought to clean it up. Big job!"

The girls nodded.

"Good gracious." Aunt Rose looked at the empty space where the bed had been. "I vow that bed hasn't been taken down in years and years." They walked over to the cardboard box.

"We were just talking about the box when you came," Edith said.

"Wonder what could be in it?"

"Looks like old papers," Samme said. "Could be a snake's nest."

"Snakes don't make nests in boxes," Edith answered. "I'm going to explore that box!"

Taking silence for consent, she knelt, digging into the papers. "Something hard." She dug on into the yellowed paper. "Red," she announced, sneezing in the dust as she uncovered a bright patch. "Glass!" Samme began to pull away the paper and together they uncovered more of the red glass.

"A lamp!" Edith exclaimed. "I think." She carefully lifted a large, red bubble of glass with copper fittings, resting it beside her. She picked up the second red bubble which was the chimney.

"Beautiful!" Aunt Rose exclaimed. "And very old. We'll take care of it until the boy can claim it."

They marveled at the crimson hue and the graceful design in the base and globe of the antique lamp.

"I recall Granny May once mentioned a red lamp. A wedding gift. I had never seen it nor did anyone else as far as I know."

Samme was disappointed. "What we needed to find

was a lot of money. Money would be a help to Jason. He doesn't need a fancy lamp."

"I have supper ready," Aunt Rose said. "We'll take the lamp home until it can be placed safely in his hands. Poor lad."

That night in bed, the girls talked.

How would it be at the cabin this minute? It would be silent and dark with little animals walking over the floor.

Would Jason find the note they had left for him? He must know about the salesman and the strangers, for hadn't they seen him watching them from the cabin doorway? Did he know why they were there? Where had he gone in the seconds it had taken the girls to get inside the cabin?

Samme sat up. Was that a sound? The cats? She turned over and went to sleep.

The next morning brought a hot breakfast and work to be done. The girls washed the dishes. Edith reached into the cupboard, putting away the dishes. She looked up on the top shelf to see the red lamp.

Her eyes widened. The spot was empty. The wonderful red glass was gone!

"Aunt Rose!" she called. Aunt Rose was loosening the ground around the new potato plants when both girls came running from the kitchen.

"Jason's lamp is gone," Edith said.

"Did you move it?" Samme asked, looking hopefully at her aunt. Aunt Rose shook her head. She leaned the hoe against the garden gate and returned to the house with the girls.

The three of them stood looking up at the empty shelf.

"Was the door locked?" Samme asked.

"No one locks doors here. It would be an insult to the neighbors."

The lamp's disappearance was a mystery. The girls raced to get through the morning's work. The beds were shaken out and straightened. With a breeze coming in every door and window the work of cleaning the house was quickly finished. Soon it was as bright and fresh as the outdoors.

The scent of green leaves and wild blossoms filled the air. The girls were glad to get their work done so they could go over to the cabin.

"Right from under our noses," Samme said.

"What?" Edith asked.

"The lamp," Samme said. "Right from under our noses."

"I've considered the whole thing," Edith said. "Who knew the lamp was here? We three. The only other person who might have known is Jason."

Samme shook her head. "Why would he steal his own lamp?"

"I don't know. Somehow I feel that the red lamp isn't far away."

Samme grunted. "It's far enough away that I can't see it."

After lunch the girls started for Granny May's cabin.

Now it seemed a friendly place to go—not just an empty building, but a place where you might meet a friend. An exciting, unusual friend. A disappearing sort of friend. One that showed up suddenly out of the darkness when needed. One that vanished just as quickly. Would the hermit boy be standing in the doorway today? Or would that salesman have prospective buyers out looking at the cabin?

The girls hurried up to the door. Everything was, in fact, the same as they had left it yesterday. The airing quilts looked brighter. The bed still lay like an iron skeleton waiting to be buried. The feather mattress lay in the same misshapen hump. The girls went to the table where they had left the note for Jason, eager to discover whether he had found it.

9. THE RED LAMP

The rocks lay in almost the same pattern the girls had placed them and the note was gone. Was there a message from the hermit boy? Edith picked up the rocks one at a time. She turned each one over in her hands as if it might reveal what had happened to their printed message.

"Here's something," Edith said. Together they looked at the one word on the underside of the third rock: CAVE!

"What does it mean?" Samme asked. "Does it mean Jason lives in a cave?"

Edith sank down onto a chair. "I wish we knew. There's only one thing that *is* clear. We'll have to find this cave and go into it."

"Us," Samme squeaked, "go into a cave? What cave? We shall have to find a cave."

"There is something about the cave that is important to the hermit boy. Why else would he print this one word?" Edith began to rub out the word "cave" even as she spoke. "This must be our secret for a little while. Somehow we shall find the cave."

"What shall we write to him?" Samme asked.

Edith considered. "One word . . . COMING! Large and clear!" Edith printed the word right on the rock where the word "cave" had been. "There." She laid the rock in the center of the table. "No one but Jason will know what that one word means."

"Caves are dark," Samme said.

"Let's get on with sweeping the cabin floor. This time we'll need water to give the boards a good scrubbing."

Samme found a battered bucket in one of the pens. They carried water into the cabin and threw small amounts of it over the floor, sweeping back and forth with the broom. Outraged spiders ran helter-skelter or swung from webs high and dry.

The chairs and pieces of chairs were set out under the trees. The drawers were taken from the chest and carried outside to be emptied. Three hairless, pink, squirming baby field mice tumbled out of a drawer in a ball of chewed wool. Samme gathered up the ball of wool, keeping the baby mice inside, and placed them gently back in the corner of the drawer. "Their mother will come back," Samme said. "These babies can live here until they are old enough to go into the woods."

One by one they carried the drawers back into the cabin. Edith swept the sides and top of the wood chest.

"I guess I really don't understand why we're doing all this work," Samme confessed. "Do you think the hermit boy will lose it all when the sale comes up?"

"There's always hope," Edith answered. "I'm going along with the thought that some way will be found to save the cabin and land."

They tugged the bed parts back into the cabin. With a rock Edith pounded the iron pins which held the rails and the head and bottom in one solid piece. The clang of the rock striking the iron bedpost echoed and reechoed through the woods. At last the huge heavy bed stood strong. They pressed the bumpy feather mattress until it was as smooth as possible.

Over the feather mattress they tucked the thinnest blanket. One by one the heavy quilts were placed on the bed. The bed did look almost as if someone intended to sleep in it.

"Put the nightgown under the quilts at the head of the bed," Samme said. "When we get the other chair repaired and set in place, it will look as if someone really lived here."

Edith frowned at the lopsided door. "Well, at least this room looks pretty good."

The sun shone with approval and the birds kept up a happy song of encouragement.

Down by the spring the girls scrubbed the last two chairs. The broom swung with short strokes, cleaning away the years' accumulation of dust and cobwebs.

The chest of drawers was shoved in place, all the drawers put in except the top one, which had crumbled. It had been carried to the junk heap.

In back of the cabin Samme found a cream-colored crock with a perky rooster painted on it in blue. She washed it and, finding a cloth about the proper size, made a doily and placed the crock on top of the chest of drawers.

"How's that?" She stood back, her hands on her hips.

"Very nice," Edith said, grinning. "You're getting to be a regular interior decorator."

Samme made a face.

As soon as the girls stepped out, a wood thrush flew in and perched on the crock.

"The birds are still coming and going as they please," Samme lamented. "The mice still are curled snugly in their woolen ball and seem as lively as ever."

"It's not everybody who has real live birds coming and going in their house and so much fresh air," Edith said.

"Nor a nest of mice in their dresser drawer," Samme said, smugly.

Time for supper came faster than expected. Gathering up their broom and dustpan, they headed for home and the sweet smell of fresh hot biscuits.

Late in the night, out of a dream, Edith awoke to the sound of singing. She sat up straight. The song was coming in the window and open door. She looked over at Samme, who was fast asleep. In bare feet she crossed over to Samme's bed. "Wake up," she whispered. "Wake up, I hear the hermit boy singing."

Samme pushed back her long hair.

"Come along," Edith said, thrusting a robe into her sister's hands.

Still barefooted, they slipped through the kitchen and out the door.

With a finger to her lips Edith silenced Samme's sleepy questions. She pointed up the hill and the musical words flowed toward them. Sharp rocks stabbed into their bare feet. Why hadn't they put on shoes?

"It's no use," Samme moaned, "I can't walk over these rocks."

"I'll go back for our shoes," Edith said, and disappeared in the darkness.

Samme tried to relax. What was there to fear? Alone on a hill in the dark? Lots of things, that's what.

Something furry was walking all around her in circles. Goose pimples stood out on her skin. Rubbing . . . purring. "Those darn cats. Pillow Paws!" Samme was mad and relieved at the same time.

"I sure am getting mixed up in a lot of foolishness,"

Samme told Pillow Paws sleepily. "Don't you ever sleep? I suppose you're asking what I'm doing sitting on the hillside in the middle of the night. Well, the answer is . . . I don't know."

"Here are your shoes," Edith whispered. "Why are you talking to yourself?"

"I wasn't talking to myself. Pillow Paws is here. We were talking, Pillow Paws and me!"

"And here are the rest of the cats," Edith said.

Holding hands, the girls started on up the hill, feeling their way. Happy for the company in the middle of the night, all the cats followed, winding in and out, purring between their feet.

"I feel silly with all these cats trailing," Edith hissed.

"Only one way to get rid of them," Samme answered. "Pour a bowl of milk and slip away while they're drinking."

It took some exploring around in the cold water of the spring to find the milk bucket. But the idea worked. The cats gathered around the bowl.

Standing beyond the barn, the girls waited, hoping the singing would begin again, and show them the way to the singer. After a few minutes they heard a new song. This time it was one they knew, "The Old Rugged Cross." They walked as far as the stump where they had placed the platter of corn bread and honey.

"Do you think we could get a little closer?" Samme whispered.

In response to Samme's question Edith took her hand. They moved forward. She caught her breath, holding tight to Samme's hand. For here was Jason, the hermit boy, blending with the shadows. He seemed to smile as he disappeared again. The girls stood still.

Then the hermit boy struck a match. There was a flash of red light, followed by a steady glow. Jason did have the red glass lamp. He lit it to show them he had it. The lamp sat on a stump, bathing the space in a red circle. The boy stood at the edge of the circle. His dark, longish hair was tinted with color. The fringes of his leather jacket swayed back and forth in the night wind. Abruptly he blew out the light, leaving total darkness. The mellow sound of bare footfalls told them he was gone.

So the hermit boy had taken the lamp. But why did he want the girls to know he had it? The whispered question was on the lips of both girls as they made their way back to the house.

The next morning they told Aunt Rose what happened so she wouldn't worry about one of those "creepers" being in her house. "I am happy that the hermit boy has the lamp," Aunt Rose said and the girls agreed.

That afternoon they were again at Granny May's cabin. Edith exclaimed over the sagging door, held up by one rusty hinge. "I wonder if this cabin will ever look like a real home? To do the job right is going to take more than a broom and a mop."

"It is beautiful here," Samme said. "Even with the cabin sagging I understand why the hermit boy loves the woods and Summer Valley so much that he hides rather than be taken away." Samme looked into her sister's face. "I'm not even wishing for a snake bite kit."

"Good," Edith exclaimed, "'cause where we're going soon you'll need all the courage you've got."

"You mean when we go to find the cave," Samme said. Her voice faltered.

Edith nodded. "After we give Jason time to find our message written on the rock."

10. NO PLACE
FOR YOUNGUNS

The next afternoon the girls hurried over the path that
was now so familiar to Granny May's cabin. They were
pleasantly surprised. The door which just yesterday
had hung on one broken hinge now hung as straight as
the door of a new cabin.

"Good grief!" Samme exclaimed. "Someone has
worked on the cabin."

"Who do you suppose it could have been?" Edith opened and closed the door just for the joy of seeing it work.

"Not Jason," Samme said. "Where would the hermit boy get new door hinges?"

"It couldn't have been Aunt Rose. We've been with her all the time since we were here yesterday."

"What about the Baron?" said a third voice.

The girls turned. There stood the Baron, lifting his brown hat up and down in greeting. He smiled through his white whiskers at their surprised faces.

"How did you know we were working on the cabin?"

"How did I know? Reckon the hills for miles around knew. All the clatter, clamor, and commotion you made pounding on that iron bed. By Fire, it made me nosey. I hiked over." The Baron replaced his hat. "Just couldn't help joining in the good work. Glad you're pleased."

"Sure are. This big room looks wonderful with a real door. We're fixing it up for the hermit boy. We want him to use it for a real home someday," Samme explained.

"Here's our next problem." Edith led the way to the lean-to kitchen. "A rat family lived in the woodbox. Take a miracle to do anything here."

"The big room looked almost that bad before we started on it," Samme pointed out.

"If it's a miracle needed," the Baron said, "I'm sure

you girls will make one. Here's something I bought in town for you girls."

Samme shrieked in delight at the sight of a bulging sack of candy bars. "Almost forgot what candy looks like. Haven't seen any since the bus trip." She tore the wrapper from a Baby Ruth and was about to take a bite. She stopped in mid-air, catching Edith's eyes; the girls nodded in wordless understanding. They put the candy back into the brown paper sack and folded the top down firmly.

"Saving the candy for something special?" the Baron asked.

"For the hermit boy."

"Jason?" The Baron's eyes opened wide.

"We'll take this candy with us when we go to find his cave."

The Baron jumped up from his seat on the log. "Cave? By Fire, the cave's no place for younguns."

"We may as well tell you," Edith said. "We have a message from the hermit boy."

"A one-word message," Samme added.

"The word CAVE," Edith continued. "Do you know which cave he could mean?"

"Somehow I'm not so surprised. There is only one cave he could have meant."

"What's the cave like?" Edith wanted to hear all about it.

"Folks hereabouts is most afraid of that cave. It's a wild place, not explored like some. And bats. By Fire, you never saw the like of bats as come out of that hole at sundown. 'Tis a black cloud of them and shrillin' to a standstill. The cold, icy air pours out with them, eerie it is with the feel of the grave. I hear tell, too, of many a heap of bones in there. I wouldn't venture back inside that cave for all the . . ."

"We think the hermit boy lives in the cave," Samme said.

The girls watched the Baron's face. Was he trying to scare them away from the cave on purpose? Did he fear they would get Jason caught by the city welfare people?

"Huh," the Baron grunted. "Nobody knows where the boy lives. That message doesn't mean the cave's his home."

The Baron sat back on the log as if preparing for a long argument. "It's jest that the cave is not a fit place to go, dangerous, a devil's hole. There's horns coming right out of the floor." He held his fingers straight up to show how the horns grew. "And horns coming right down from the ceiling to stab a fellow through." He held his other hand with fingers downward to show the girls and fixed them with a stern look.

"Stalactites and stalagmites," Edith announced, from the store of book reading. "Stalactites hang from the ceiling, stalagmites form on the floor of the caves and grow upward."

"How's that?" the Baron asked.

Samme looked impressed.

The Baron went on talking. "Bears and fox, wolves, in there, too, and a passel of bobcats most likely. Deep down, way back, there's just herds of slick, hungry, blind, giant lizards . . . and don't reckon 'cause they're blind they can't find . . ." He rolled his eyes toward heaven, then looked to see what effect his words had on the two girls.

Samme paled but remained silent, waiting to hear what her sister had to say.

"Salamanders," Edith announced as if she were reading from a book. "They grow to be six inches long and are harmless. They eat only tiny insects."

The Baron pushed his hat back on his head and stared at the toe of his shoe. "Strange I hear so many tales of hogs and cows disappearin' right in the neighborhood of that cave, what you say to that?"

Edith winked at Samme. "I say you're only trying to scare us."

Samme, picking up courage, spoke. "We're going." Edith tried a different approach. "If you were going cave exploring, what would you take with you?"

"Which I ain't," the Baron announced. "By Fire, I'm not at an age for such foolishness, but just sayin' I was I would take a long stout rope or two if I had 'em, corn bread and beans a-plenty, matches in a dry pouch, candles, flashlight if I could get hold a one and a real warm coat. The deep parts is mighty cold I reckon."

"We'll be careful," Edith promised.

"Maybe we won't go into the cave at all." Samme eyed her sister hopefully. "May stay right at the edge. Might be a cozy room right at the front with the floor all covered with feathers and soft moss. We would just sit there inside the door."

"Mind you do," the Baron said.

The directions the Baron at last gave the girls to get to the cave were simple enough.

The next day they were standing at the point of the V where Summer Valley ended. The cabin of Granny May's was the only cabin, the only building they had passed. It wasn't far beyond the cabin that the valley ended. After passing the cabin the girls had followed a ravine, then climbed up the rough, overgrown sides. Now they were standing close to where the mouth of the cave must be. The smooth valley ceased to be and sprang almost straight up into a tree-and-vine-covered hill. The only color they saw besides green was the white of huge rock outcroppings jutting from the hill. They knew the opening of the cave was near one of those rocks. How long would it take to find it?

The girls rested, surveying the forbidding hill. "I read about caves in a book," Edith said. "There was this one cave in New York—Howe's Cave, it was called. A cow found that cave."

"A cow?" Samme exclaimed. "Good grief, if a cow can find a cave, I guess we can!"

"The cow's name was Millicent."

"Millicent—what a name for a cow. How did she find the cave?"

"Well, where this cow lived the summers were very hot. Every day the cow would go to this one special spot in the pasture and just stand there. She did this over and over and the farmer became curious."

"Farmers are a curious lot," Samme said.

" 'Why does my good cow Millicent always stand in one spot in the pasture?' the farmer asked himself." Edith paused for the story to take effect.

"Well?" Samme urged.

"So the farmer went out to stand on the spot himself. He discovered why Millicent stood there day after day in the hot summer. Cool, lovely cool air was coming out of the ground. The mystery of Millicent's behavior was solved. The cow had discovered the opening of a great cave."

"That makes it simple for us. All we have to do is wait for a very hot day; walk over the countryside until we find a cow . . ."

"Don't be smart," Edith said.

"I really do have a way," Samme said. "Just go up there and find a cold rock."

"A cold rock? You think the cave mouth will be near it and the cold air from the cave will make the rock cool. . . ."

Samme nodded. "Don't put it just that way. Do you have to say cave's mouth? Makes me feel as if I'm to be swallowed up—yes, come on, let's start."

"Just a minute. Caves are carved out of rock by groundwater; the books say so. We must look for water, a small waterfall perhaps or a spring on the hillside—there are so many springs in the Ozarks."

"I know just how to find springs or waterfalls in places where you can't see right down to the ground," Samme said. "And I didn't read it in a book. The Baron told me." Samme had always waited for a time like this when she could tell Edith something for a change.

"How?" Edith said. "Just tell me how you know from way down here that there's water up there. You can't see anything but vines, rocks and trees."

"The secret is this," Samme said proudly. "You watch the birds. Birds know where water is. When you see birds going down into a place like that time after time, you'll know they've found water even though you can't see the water."

"Seems reasonable," Edith said. "Let's watch."

Two red-winged blackbirds disappeared into the greenery above as the girls watched, followed quickly by several more. In a group, singing tweet-tweet-tweet a dozen or more gray-breasted marsh sparrows flew downward, disappearing in the same area. Several tiny wrens followed.

The girls began climbing, pushing past the branches, crawling under vines and over roots. "Look." Edith pointed to a small, smooth pathway and here they stopped to peek into a large burrow. Freshly dug earth was scattered about the hole, and an animal path led upward at a slant in the direction the birds had taken.

"Must be their path to the water," Samme said. "We just have to follow their trail." It was exciting sharing a path with wild animals and they had to crawl along with their noses almost on the ground as the way was low and narrow.

"Stay close," Edith said as she moved ahead.

Samme nodded. With the cave in mind she was going to stay close to her sister today of all days.

"You hear flowing water?" Edith said. Samme listened. A bubbling of water and a flutter of wings could be heard faintly.

"I'm a little shaky about that cave," Samme said. Then she paused to listen for the trickle of unseen water.

"Do you think the stories about bears asleep in caves and hidden treasures and . . . and piles of bones are true?"

Edith pushed aside some thick brush and fanned the gnats from her face. "A few of the stories may be true. Most are just made-up stories, productions of imagination." She crept along the trail. Samme stayed close. They came to an opening.

A tiny waterfall tinkled just on the other side of a jagged rock. Fern-covered smaller rocks strung out in steps down the hillside. Birds dipped and dived; some, very wet, sat in patches of silver sunlight drying.

Hollows in the rocks caught the overflow of the rushing streamlet, forming dozens of bird bathtubs.

11. FAITH IN
THE HERMIT BOY

"Let's just stay here," Samme said, gazing at the tranquil scene. "I like it here."

A pebble rolled. The feathered bathers flew to sunny spots higher up. There were no animal tracks here on the decaying leaves and smooth white rocks.

Edith rinsed her hands and face in the cold water. "Brrr-r-r."

"Cold as if it came from a . . . cave?" Samme questioned.

"I'll say, or underground river."

"Underground what?"

"River."

"You never mentioned anything about rivers being in caves before."

"Didn't get to it. Lots of caves have underground rivers."

"Deep?"

"Deep rivers and shallow rivers, too. Just depends."

"I suppose plenty of those pale, slimy lizards live in the rivers, too," Samme said grimly.

"Now don't talk yourself into worrying before anything happens," Edith cautioned. "We aren't even in the cave yet; besides, the lizards are only . . ."

"Six inches long," Samme cut in.

"And aren't lizards in the strictest sense but salamanders."

"Lizarders, gizzards. Salamanders scare me even more . . . and six inches is plenty long enough to suit me; enough six-inchers could eat us down to the bone —why I've heard of a three-inch fish in South American rivers that eats whole cows and . . ."

"Piranha is the name of the fish you're thinking of. South America is a long way from the Ozarks." Edith stood up, looking around the sharp rock. "What's this?

It's a strip of wool from one of the quilts we threw away. One of the quilts from Granny May's cabin."

The girls struggled around the damp rock, pulling at the faded strip of cloth. As they pulled, an opening appeared as the brush parted. "The cave entrance!" Edith exclaimed. "The hermit boy put this piece of wool here to help us find it."

Together they stared into the doorlike entrance. One side was solid rock, the other hard, red clay. Cold, refreshing air bathed their faces. They were unable to see anything but darkness on the inside because of the brightness outside.

"Where are all the bats?" Samme whispered. "I've always heard where there were caves, there were bats."

"We'll tie one end of the rope you're carrying to the rope I have and hold onto it as we walk into the cave," Edith said. "The other rope I have we'll carry with us to use later. The bats are asleep somewhere in the cave. They come out at sundown."

"Wish I could see something besides darkness," Samme said as she peered into the moist black hole. A trickle of water came out of one side of the cave entrance.

Taking a deep breath, the girls moved into the narrow corridor, glad now that they had brought heavy sweaters.

Here was a cleft in the cave wall. Did it reach far back? Was there anything in it except shadows? As their eyes began to adjust to the dimness they made out this space in the rock. Was the bottom littered with . . .

bones? It was! Samme's hand sought and gripped her sister's. Together they leaned down, enjoying the keen thrill of discovery. The bones, bare and dry, were of different sizes and shades from white to yellowed brown.

Edith slid the rope a few inches between her fingers. "Light a candle," she whispered. Why did she whisper instead of saying it out loud? The silence was so heavy she dared not break it.

Nevertheless a rolling, thunderous whisper rolled back to the girls from somewhere in the depths of the cave.

"Light a candle . . . light a candle . . . light a candle!"

Samme froze with the match in her hand poised above the candle.

Edith spoke softly. "It's only an echo. Go ahead, light the candle."

Samme came to life, touching the match to the candle. The sound of each word was flung back from the depths of the nothing darkness. As if a word-throwing giant lurked below.

Samme handed the lighted candle to Edith and replaced the lid on the box of a dozen Christmas candles which she carried. The girls cheered up as the flame grew. Now they could see where they were stepping. Their long, thin, jerky shadows climbed the gray wall. They moved on, hearing the trickle of unseen water.

"The road to nowhere," Samme said.

They moved on, at once protected and held prisoner of the enclosing wall of the corridor. After a timeless space of walking between the walls which reflected the flickering candle, the walls disappeared.

As far as the candlelight reached there was emptiness. The only solid thing was the hard surface beneath their feet.

In front of the girls was the very thing the Baron had warned them against. "Teeth!" Samme cried. "Just like the Baron said." The teeth, blunt and thick, stood up from the floor. Long, sharp teeth came down from above to meet the bottom ones.

They stood close together in the gray, forbidding . . .

Edith reached out to touch one of the unmovable formations.

"What did you say they were?" Samme asked. Her voice no longer echoed.

"To think that we're seeing these with our very own eyes and right on the spot where they've grown." Edith's voice was soft with the wonder of it. "Stalactites grow down, stalagmites grow up. They're natural formations created by the slow dripping of water and the drying of water. The water leaves limestone deposits which build up from the floor and down from the ceiling. Can you imagine the time it takes one of these large ones to form? Thousands of years."

Samme reached out and ran her hand over a hard gray tooth.

"Look here!" Edith exclaimed. "Two have met, forming a column. A stone post."

In the wee circle of light Samme didn't look pleased. "Looks to me like we're taking the road from nowhere into nothing, or walking straight into a dragon's mouth. Or is this the mouth of a giant salamander?"

"You mustn't imagine all those dreadful things," Edith said. "Everything's fine. See, I have the rope we tied to the tree right here in my hand. We can follow it back to the entrance when we're ready to go."

"I'm ready. I'm ready," Samme quavered.

"Don't you have faith in the hermit boy? He knows we're in the cave. I believe he's near and knows we're safe."

"If he is near, I wish he'd turn on the lights," Samme said. "Well, it's on into the dragon's mouth for us." She attempted to sound cheerful.

"Let's tie the rope you're carrying to this one. It's about run out." Edith took the end of the ropes and began tying them, looping the rope she had taken from Samme over her arm. "Sorry you came?"

Samme shook her head. "I'm scared, but I wouldn't have missed it for anything."

They stepped into the dragon's mouth, pushing through the black forest of cold stone stumps. Some grew so close together that the girls could just squeeze between them. The loop of the rope Edith dragged behind to mark their passage caught on the upthrust stalagmites. She gave the rope a firm tug to be sure it held; it was their lifeline for the return trip.

It was colder here than it had been in the corridor and, if possible, darker. Edith helped Samme over an especially rough spot, squinting in the dancing candle-light, wondering what new adventure lay ahead.

Samme fastened the top button of her heavy sweater, dodging a low-hanging stalactite which threatened to scrape off the top of her head. They struggled on into the darkness. The candle glowed, making a moon of pale light around their feet.

Edith paused to take two fresh candles from the box. It was reassuring to see that nine still remained. How long did it take an average candle to burn down? She should have found that out before entering the cave. It would have been a good way to tell time. She handed a blazing candle to Samme and held her own high, like an underground Statue of Liberty.

"A curtain!" Samme exclaimed. "A stone curtain." The girls stopped to study this new wonder.

" 'Dripstone' it's called," Edith said. "It's a limestone sheet that hangs from the roof of caves, curtain-like."

She was pleased that she'd read about caves this past year so she could at least give familiar names to these strange surroundings.

Edith tugged Samme forward, vowing not to let go of her hand. Their goal was the dripstone curtain.

Finally they stood within reach of the thin, hard barrier. There was a narrow black opening. To enter or not to enter. That was the question. Edith let out another length of rope. They walked up to the curtain, and touched it.

"What's on the other side?" Samme whispered.

"Let's find out." Edith drew Samme after her through the black opening.

The girls stood quiet, their backs touching the cold of the stone curtain. Out of the total darkness ahead came a red glow. It could come from only one thing, the red lamp. Where the red lamp was, Jason would be. For the first time since entering the cave the girls felt safe.

"Blow out your candle," Edith directed, "but keep a match in your hand for relighting." She blew out her own candle at the same time. The darkness seemed thick enough to slice. The red glow seemed to grow in all its glory, its beauty enhanced by the black velvet surroundings.

The girls waited.

"We may be able to see into the red light with our candles out," Edith whispered. They looked hard, hoping to see the boy. They were still alone!

"We'll have to light the candles again to make our way to the red lamp."

"Jason means it as a guide to us," Samme said. The light of the two candles flared and the girls moved forward with slow, searching steps.

The long rope was giving out. Would it let them reach the lamp? They dared not go beyond the rope's length.

Now they were bathed in the red, walking in a globe of color; they had reached the room of the lamp.

They stood before the entrance, an opening the size of a wagon wheel. The girls peered into the red room. The air coming from it was warm and dry, a great contrast to the damp, chilling air of the cave. The room was small and cozy. Samme could wait no longer. She crawled over the rim of the stone circle and went inside.

Edith followed. No wonder the room was warm. A crude fireplace stood at one end. Stone stools were placed around the room. A narrow rock ledge with two folded quilts seemed to be a bed. A fire was burning in the fireplace. At first they had not seen the glow of the coals because everything else was red from the lamplight. Edith sank down on one of the stools and discovered it was soft, covered with fur.

"It's as if we were awake in a strange dream," Samme said. "I feel as if I were in someone's private apartment!"

"You are!"

Framed in a narrow entrance which the girls had not noticed before was the hermit boy of Summer Valley.

Jason was straight and motionless, his face as stern as an Indian's. Samme imagined that Daniel Boone might have looked just this way in his youth. Jason's feet were bare and he wore the same yellowed gold leather jacket which they had glimpsed before.

He smiled, his face changing into a friendly welcome.

"I was watching to see that you made it through the mouth." He moved to the center of the room almost without a motion and as silently as an owl flies.

Samme was the first to speak. Even this unusual young man could not awe her into silence for long.

"Good grief! I was scared to death. Thank goodness

you're here." Then looking from side to side she said, "Where are the salamanders? I'm hungry."

The smile on Jason's tanned face broadened to a grin. "I don't think the salamanders are good to eat. . . ."

"I didn't intend to eat the salamanders!" Samme cried in alarm. "Just wanted to make sure they weren't underfoot. I don't want to eat them, I don't want them to eat me." She took a step closer. "Will you sing for us again? We have food with us." There were so many things she wanted to say and ask now that the boy was near at last.

Edith regained her speech if only to bring Samme's to a halt and to restore order. "First things first," she announced, sounding for all the world like Aunt Rose. She dug into the pack at her feet. "Food."

This was a topic on which they all agreed. The blanket tablecloth was laid before the fireplace and the largest portions placed before Jason. He sat on his haunches easily, and gazed with unconcealed eagerness at the hickory-nut cookies and hearty sandwiches. The girls were pleased they had brought so many. Finally there were the candy bars that the Baron had brought from town. The boy took his up tenderly, sniffing the rich chocolate.

All the while Edith was thinking. *What about money to save the cabin? Was the safe in the cave?*

"That red light is giving me the creeps," Samme said, breaking the silence in her usual outspoken way.

"Me, too." The boy put the last bit of a cookie in his

mouth, rising. "I lit it for you to see the way. To let you know I was here. We don't need it now." He went over to the lamp and blew out the flame.

12. IN THE CAVE

The yellow blaze from the fireplace now cast a golden glow over the room. Jason moved on to the far corner. He reached overhead, pulling a thick vine; sunlight streamed in from above in a long tubular shape, spreading out at the bottom. "There's a trapdoor at the top, lets the sunlight in certain hours during the day." From a pile of thick chunks of black oak the boy selected one and laid it on the low fire. He stirred the hot ashes and a flame shot up.

"To think," Samme said, "that I worried about you freezing to death in the wintertime. Where does the smoke go? Someone might see it."

"Straight up and out. There's a fissure in the rocks," Jason said. "I use dry wood which makes very little smoke. Not enough to notice from the outside. I cook here and a small blaze keeps the room dry and warm."

"Are we the first to be down here and see this room?"

Jason nodded. "There are reasons. I thought a lot about it. I felt I could trust you. I want news of my father. And the last few days I've seen strangers around the cabin. I thought you might be able to tell me about them."

The girls explained to Jason about the coming sale of the cabin and land. Jason paced back and forth. They told him about his father being lost overseas. They asked about the safe.

Jason's gray eyes darkened and lines of thought grew across his smooth forehead. "There is a safe. It has money in it. I don't know how much, never needed money. I moved it down here after Granny May died. . . . She told me to."

"If the money owed on the cabin could be paid, whatever else happened, you would still have your home," Edith said seriously.

"Come with me," Jason said.

The girls joined him as trustingly as he had accepted

their friendship. They followed him out of the cozy room into the unknown cavelike tunnels.

He led them through a narrow opening hardly more than a slit in the damp wall of rock. From a ledge above the boy took a length of wood, the end of which was wrapped with strips of fiber. He dipped the fiber end into a stone crock, then touched a match to it. The exploding blaze sent light dancing in every direction. The glare caught each twisted shape of stone in a bright grip, releasing it as they passed. Weird, eerie growths in limestone hovering above and beside them kept the girls close to their tall friend. They followed him along uneven paths, tight, gray alleys.

Jason slowed his steps so that the girls might stay up with his long strides. This underground path which was familiar to him left them cold with fear. Only trust in their new friend gave the girls courage. It was clear that these dark trails and mysterious tunnels were as familiar to the hermit boy as the sunny walks in the forest above.

"Truth is surely stranger than fiction," Edith murmured. "If you don't think so, just try telling this to our friends at home when we return."

"Look at me." Samme said, hanging onto Edith's shirt. "I'm a two-legged mole."

Edith looked into Samme's brooding face. "How do you feel?"

"Well, I don't feel good." Before Samme could list her complaints and her wishes for a sunny patch of green grass, a gigantic chamber opened before them.

The boy paused, his shadow swaying as he moved the torch so the girls might see some part of the vast cavern in which they stood. He turned. "Are you afraid?"

"For the first time in my life I can't talk," Samme said. "Well, not much."

"It's as safe here as in the forest above," the boy assured them. "I've been this way many times. I've removed the roughest barriers and shored up the narrowest pathways."

They moved on, turning from the endless space of the mighty room into a side tunnel. Here ledges at different heights gave the appearance of never-ending shelves. The distant sound of falling water filled the hall with musical undertones. The tunnel widened into a hall, in the center of which was a circular pool. The firelight of the torch fell on the pool, showing the water to be a clear blue.

"It's . . . it's pretty here," Edith ventured, relieved, thinking of the vast reaches and strange disturbing ways which they had just come.

"What's back there?" Samme asked, pointing a finger toward the unseen, vast space beyond.

"Bats, spiders and cave rats . . . and danger," Jason replied, smiling. "Walk behind me, I'll show you." Keeping the light high, he went forward.

A blackness deeper than the dark of a moonless night tore open before the light. The orange-yellow glow revealed huge, sharp masses of stone hung suspended in serpentlike shapes over bottomless pits.

Edith wanted to cover her ears, for it looked as if the

eels of stone and crystal might at any minute lose their hold and tumble out of sight, out of the world. Both girls shivered.

Dogtooth crystals sparkled in rainbow colors as the torchlight touched the minerals.

"Even here there is beauty when the light shines," Edith breathed.

A doomed ceiling roofed the fearful, rugged depths in the caves, awing the group into silence. Secretive passages slid off in a dozen different directions. Glittering needles of quartz lined the cavities. On beyond could be seen the shoe-polish gleam of turbulent water.

"Beyond that water is the main entrance of this cave," Jason said. He gestured with the torch over the pits. "You can see why this has remained a wild, unexplored cave. Tough to get into if you don't know the small entrance I've made on the hillside. You came in with a rope for a guide and played it safe all the way just like real cave explorers."

His approval pleased the girls.

Then he said, "Let's return to the shelves." He didn't have to repeat the words; with one last glance at the black depths they hurried to the friendlier hall and its fanciful trimmed shelves.

They welcomed the sight of the tiny pool and the smooth floor underfoot.

"Come," said Jason. "I have something else for you to see. My best friend up to now. You'll understand why I need warmer-natured friends when you meet him."

"Him?" Edith asked.

"Lost John."

Samme looked around. "Someone else is here?" It was a strange name with fearful omens.

Jason grinned. "Named him myself. Been here with me since I found him. Come along. There's no harm in the dead."

Intending to reassure his new friends, Jason didn't realize that his words had exactly the opposite effect.

Edith followed Jason, trying to look brave for Samme's sake. Samme followed, not daring to be left alone and yet not anxious to meet Jason's strange friend. They trailed the light and their leader, wondering what was to happen next.

They stopped before a wall where dripping water had carved a coffinlike hollow. Jason held the light before the opening.

"Edith and Samme, be pleased to meet my friend, Lost John. John, these are my new and trusted friends, Edith and Samme." He made the introduction, looking full of mischief.

The girls stared mutely at a skeleton.

"An Indian," Jason said.

The skeleton lay in a circle, skull and kneebones touching. The cracked arm bones were folded under a sharp chin. He was grinning, wide and permanently and forever. A few teeth had dropped from the jaw and lay nearby.

"A bit thin, isn't he?" Samme croaked.

"Little wonder," Jason answered. "I figure he's laid there maybe a thousand years without a bite to eat."

The boy dribbled fine limestone through his fingers. Some of it fell into Lost John's hollow eye sockets. Jason brushed it away carefully.

"I found him under a rock where he had fallen, gathered up the pieces and brought him to my museum. Can you work puzzles? Here are his small bones. I didn't know just where they fit, so I laid them together."

The girls peered over their new friend's shoulder at Lost John's small bones lying in a neat pile. Some were rib bones and the rest anyone's guess.

"Where did you find him?"

Jason pointed away into the darkness. "Deeper in there are many tunnels and large rooms, some almost as large as Summer Valley. From the tools, utensils and weapons I found I knew he had made this cave his home. He may have fallen to his death from the high ledge above where I found him. He was almost covered with limestone. I spotted his axe first. Then the finger bones. I dug him out and brought him here."

Edith shook her head at this likeable boy who had lived such an unusual life. At the ease with which he made his home in this unhospitable place.

"Come," he said, "see my shelves."

"No more Lost Johns," Samme said.

"I promise."

So they followed again back to the hall of shelves and the small pool. As Jason raised the light, the girls could see that the shelves held many things.

"Stone points," Jason said. "Arrowheads." He held

the fine, sharp hunting heads low so that they might get a close look. There were pots, dishes and other containers. "The bowl which holds oil for the torch came from here."

Some of the vases and pots were decorated with stiff animal figures and geometric designs. Jason's face beamed with the joy of sharing his treasures as he pointed out different pieces to the girls, sometimes taking one down so that they might see it better.

"Been gathering these since I can remember, and Granny before me. She led me through the tunnels in the cave when I was small. When she knew she was going to die"—Jason's voice softened—"she told me to come in here. That folks might try to take me away. She was against that. This cave was Granny May's and her father's before her."

The talk of Granny May brought Edith's thought back to the reason they had ventured into the cave in the first place.

"Samme and I want to help you keep the cabin and all that goes with it. So do all the hill people. That real estate salesman who has been showing your cabin feels certain the whole thing is as good as his."

The boy's lean body tightened. "It's the first time in all these years a city stranger has set foot on Granny's place."

"How much money is in the safe?" Samme asked.

As if he had reached a decision, the boy set down the utensil he had been holding and reached for the flaming torch. Motioning for the girls to follow, he led the way back through the great halls and along the narrow paths. Soon they were in the cozy room where the girls had first seen the red lamp. Jason smothered the fire of the torch and laid it, smoldering, in one corner. He knelt down on the floor and began lifting one of the group of flat stones. With a clatter he thrust it aside, reaching into the space beneath. Then he pulled out a boxlike container.

Brushing dirt from the top, he set it before the girls. The door had a wooden knob and beneath that a small drawer. The whole thing was somewhat larger than a breadbox.

"The safe!" Samme exclaimed.

Coins rattled as the boy pried open the drawer. A tiny lady's watch on a delicate chain slid into view and a few dim pictures of people in old-fashioned clothes.

He tugged open the door, scooping with his hands. He dropped green bills, coins and broken jewelry in a jumbled heap upon the stones.

13. A SURPRISE OPENING

Jason leaned over the clutter, brushed away the money and picked up a brooch. The setting was dark with age, the clasp rusty with the passage of time. He polished the pale stone by rubbing it up and down on his leather jacket. "Granny May's," he said, then he picked up a tarnished, worn wedding band. "She had me bring all this down here before she died." The girls stared a moment in silence with the hermit boy. He lay the brooch beside the scattered money. "She told me to use it when the need came."

"We must count the money," Edith said. She and Samme and Jason began laying the bills in separate piles. There was a silence broken only by the faint rustle of the bills swishing through anxious hands.

Three pair of troubled eyes stared down at the money.

"Five-hundred thirty-five dollars," Edith said.

"Not enough." Samme looked from Edith to Jason and again at the stack of bills.

"Take what's here," Jason said as if he had made a sudden and final decision. "Take the jewelry, too. Ask your Aunt Rose if the value of the jewelry might be enough to make up the difference." He took a leather pouch from over the fireplace.

Samme held the pouch open while Edith gathered up the bills and the jewelry, putting them in the pouch. She drew the string tight. A silence followed as each of them considered what had been done and what was yet to come. The tall boy gazed quietly up into the gleam of sunlight.

They left the cave room by a new route which slanted downward. After walking perhaps ten minutes they began to climb along a steep grade. A tough length of grapevine was lashed along one side and holding onto this made the climb easier. At the top was a landing, Jason stopped and reached above his head. He was opening or unlatching something. He pushed up, and a beam of light made the girls blink. He climbed out of the opening and helped Samme out first. Edith heard her gasp of surprise.

She took the strong hand Jason reached down to her as he pulled her up into the full light of day beside Samme.

The girls found themselves standing in the big room of Granny May's cabin. The opening that led down into Jason's cozy retreat in the depths of the earth was in the floor.

Jason laid the boards on the trapdoor back into place. They blended into the floor.

"So this is how you get out of sight so fast. This is where you disappeared the day we saw you at the door."

The boy laughed. "You two are the first to know about this trapdoor."

The girls were proud of Jason's trust in them. First the money and now the secret of the trapdoor. They stayed out of sight in the cabin until Jason motioned that all was clear.

"Come back soon," he said, instead of good-bye. His eyes told them how much he had enjoyed their company and how sorry he was they must go.

"I'll take care of your rope and anything else you have left in the cave."

"Thank you," Edith said. "One of the ropes belongs to you. Thank you for helping us that dreadful night when Samme fell in the pit."

"Yes," Samme added, "and for guiding us to Aunt Rose's house."

"You're welcome," Jason smiled. He reached up to the rafter above and brought down a horn, the natural, hollow-pointed horn of a large animal. "If you need me," he said, "open this trapdoor and blow the horn. One blast means you're coming in and two blasts means I should come to you." Waving, he lifted the trapdoor and disappeared from sight.

Samme sat down on a chair beside the plank table.

"Tired?" Edith asked.

Samme shook her head. Two round tears ran down her cheeks. "It's just that I don't want Jason to have to go down into that hole any more. I wish he would come up here and stay."

"The room Jason has in the cave isn't exactly a hole," Edith said cheerfully. "And what boy wouldn't envy his adventures? Wasn't he proud showing us the stone pots and the other things on the shelves? The way he's trusted us today with his money and the jewelry, I'm sure he will soon learn to trust other people."

Samme wiped her eyes, nodding.

When they arrived back home at Aunt Rose's, she noticed the leather pouch at once. Her dark eyes asked the question and Edith answered. "Oh, Aunt Rose, you won't believe . . ."

"She will, she will. . . ." Samme cried eagerly. "We've found the hermit boy. Tell Aunt Rose, Edith! Hurry! And tell about all those pots and tools and strange old relics."

"It's true," Edith held up the leather pouch. "And the money from Granny May's safe is in this pouch and the jewelry, too. Jason said you might find out the value of the jewelry."

"This is wonderful," Aunt Rose cried. "More than I dared hope for. The truth is I do have some other business in town that needs attending to and perhaps I could see about the value of the jewelry at the same time. The Grove's boy. You know the people with the telephone. He takes me into town when I need to go which isn't often. They are so kind that way. Of course,"—Aunt Rose smiled, her eyes sparkling—"I did help the two youngest Grove children into the world."

"The hermit boy helps a lot of people, too," Samme said happily.

"And now a lot of people are going to help him."

"You bet your boots they are," Aunt Rose said.

So that was settled. The girls splashed water as they washed, only now remembering that the largest part of the food they had taken for lunch had gone to their tall friend in the cozy room in the cave. "You should have seen him eat," Samme said.

"And now you girls had better eat, too," Aunt Rose said. She placed a large salad on the table of fresh crisp garden lettuce with slivers of red radish and yellow carrots in it. The sweet fruit smell of hot berry pies filled the air. What a wonderful pie baker Aunt Rose was.

The next day dawned bright and beautiful, the long rays of new sun streaking the hills and Summer Valley with golden ribbons.

Aunt Rose had ridden Job, the mule, to the mailbox on the main road and picked up the paper. She laid it out wide on the polished table. Three busy heads bowed over the paper, seeking news about the tax sale. There it was. It listed the time and the place was Jason's cabin. Aunt Rose's dark serious eyes met those of Samme and Edith.

"A week from tomorrow," Edith said slowly.

"And tomorrow is Saturday." Both girls looked at Aunt Rose.

Aunt Rose made a little tent out of her fingers, thinking. "I saw the Grove's boy at the mailbox. I shan't be able to go into town until next Friday. The day before the sale. The boy has sent for a part to the car." She paused and her lips pressed in a firm line. She put her arms around the girls. "Between you girls and the Baron and all the good people somehow we'll save the cabin and land for Jason."

"We sure will," Samme said. "That's for the old sale." Samme put her thumbs in her ears and wagged her fingers making Aunt Rose and Edith laugh in spite of themselves.

Then a new sound came to their ears. Far up on the county road they heard the sound of a motor. The motor stopped abruptly.

"Car stopped on the county road," Aunt Rose said. "They have to walk a way through the woods to get down here, as you girls well know from the first day when Henry brought you. If Henry had come in from the other way he might have let you off at the county road instead of the old empty house but it's still a good walk either way."

"Then we are going to have a visitor," Edith said.

"Who could it be?" Samme and Edith went to the door, looking off down the path and across the creek past the log bridge. Aunt Rose poured coffee and stirred in fresh cream.

Some time passed with just the sound of singing birds in the air. Aunt Rose went to stand behind the girls at the door. In another fifteen minutes they heard the sound of voices.

Aunt Rose looked. What she saw caused her good-natured face to turn sour and crooked. Who were these unwelcome strangers?

"That Mrs. Dinliddy again," Aunt Rose gritted.

The women approaching were all dressed up, plainly not hill folks. One, thin as a cane, was buttoned into a frilly blue-and-white checked suit. On her head was a pillbox hat of the same material.

The second woman looked powerful enough to pull a team of mules laden with iron ore out of the swamp. She had the air of a general preparing to strike a civilizing blow onto a village of cannibals. Stiff-kneed, her arms bent in at the elbow, she led the charge. In a tight grip she held a walking stick, which she waved as she talked, which seemed to be most of the time. The stick lashed the air as her mouth opened and shut.

A hardy looking man in outdoor clothes plodded after the women. He looked as if he wished he were somewhere else. He mopped his perspiring face with a big red handkerchief.

Aunt Rose certainly wasn't going to put the coffee pot on for these three. The girls couldn't blame her. From the looks of them they spelled nothing but trouble.

The deep, rasping voice of the heavy woman, Mrs. Dinliddy, reached their ears. "This is the fourth trip into this endless wilderness in as many weeks. If that boy isn't found soon, we're going to be laughed out of the county. It's your duty, Sheriff, to see that this doesn't happen."

Now they could see the gleaming metal star on the man's jacket. The sheriff, red in the face, squinted and looked up Summer Valley. The woman talked on.

"As the most important law enforcement officer in this county . . ."

"Yes, ma'am."

"As the man whose duty it is to keep order in the county . . ."

"Yes, ma'am."

"As a man with deputies to help in cases such as this . . ."

"Yes, ma'am."

"It's been in all the papers, Sheriff." Mrs. Dinliddy turned, shaking her finger under the man's nose.

Close to the house now, she turned her ire on Aunt Rose. "A hill country full of people and no one . . . not one, mind you, will tell us where that boy is hiding. Won't raise a hand to catch and civilize him. I've tried to get you hill folks to help, to cooperate. To lay some kind of trap to catch him. Poor lad, he doesn't know what's best for him. Starving alone in the forest. Freezing in the cold winter."

Samme poked Edith in the ribs. Mrs. Dinliddy gave her a piercing glare. "What befalls that lad will be on your heads. My conscience is clear." Mrs. Dinliddy placed her hand over her heart, turning her eyes heavenward.

The thin lady in blue-and-white checks spoke. Her voice was honey sweet. "We have come to you today to appeal, to beg you to assist in the matter of locating this orphan hermit boy."

"These hillbillies are a heartless bunch. It's no good trying to get along with them, Sybil," Mrs. Dinliddy broke in. "I say strike now. That is, have the sheriff strike at once."

The sheriff cringed. He polished his star with his red handkerchief. He shifted his weight from one foot to the other as if there were hot coals in his boots.

Aunt Rose bit her tongue, to keep back angry words, but failed. "I wouldn't help you if I could," she muttered.

"Just what I expected," Mrs. Dinliddy shrilled. "Sheriff"—she waved her cane before his face—"do your duty, man, do your duty." She snorted, "Speak up. Speak up." She pushed the sheriff forward.

"Madam, I did agree to come with these . . . ladies. This is the sixth place we've stopped today, trying to pick up a trace of that kid. I'm fed up with this here situation. The papers got the story spread all over the U.S.A. Starting tomorrow a deputy is to be posted at

Granny May's cabin. We got to lay for that kid until he's found and turned over to the juvenile authorities. There's another problem. The rumors of hidden money. May or may not be true, but loafers and no-gooders is filtering into these hills, I hear. It bodes no good for property owners in these parts!"

Aunt Rose's eyes sparked fire. Her words snapped like dry twigs breaking. "I am ashamed of you, Sheriff. You a hillman, talkin' about our boy Jason that way. Frettin' about rumors, nervous as an old maid when the sun goes down. Who was it gathered black cherry bark and delivered it so's Old Minnie could make your baby throat syrup. You have a short memory, Sheriff, and you're goin' against Granny May's boy Jason for she's the very one who brought you into this world. Isn't that so, Sheriff? It's no wonder you are standing there lookin' as miserable as a coyote with his hind leg caught in a trap. Now be off, the lot of you, get off this property 'fore the buckshot starts to fly."

14. PLANS AFOOT

The two women sped down the path followed by the red-faced sheriff. Aunt Rose went into the house. There she paced back and forth, upturning the black-and-white braided rugs.

"Have we done wrong?" she said half to herself and

half-talking to the girls. "We wouldn't do the boy harm for anything in the world. Myself or the Baron, Old Minnie, who he's brought winter wood to, the Henrys and all the others." Aunt Rose raised her bowed head. "We feel as if Jason May were our own kin, but if Mrs. Dinliddy or the sheriff find Jason, how can we prevent them from taking him away?" Aunt Rose paused in her pacing. "How could we hill folks help send that boy off to the city? It would be the same as taking a fish out of water." Aunt Rose went out the door and, as the girls watched she took up the hoe fiercely and headed for the weeds in the garden with a gleam in her eye.

"The garden is Aunt Rose's thinking place," Samme said.

Edith agreed.

"And I know what you and I must do right now."

Samme looked at Edith, reading her thoughts. "Go to Granny May's cabin?"

"We must warn Jason about the deputy coming, tell him that even if the jewelry is worth enough to pay for the taxes the state could still take him away."

The walk to Granny May's cabin seemed longer than usual because their spirits were so low. As they neared the cabin, they heard the sound of angry voices. Four people were near the door—the Baron, the salesman, and the couple.

"That man's trying to sell the cabin and land again," Samme whispered.

The Baron and the salesman were arguing. The old Baron was waving his brown hat. "You're a rascal, pretending this place is already yours. Deceivin' these folks with your talk. This cabin and land still belong to the boy Jason May up to the day of the sale. You've no right settin' foot on't."

The other man's round, soft face was flushed with heat and anger. "Look here, old timer, this place is just as good as mine." He held up both hands to keep off the Baron's striking hat. "Mine to sell or not to sell as I please."

The salesman turned to the bewildered couple with him. "Just pay no mind to this old fellow, folks." He tapped his head. "Take a good look at this rustic cabin set amid nature's wonders. A fine home for you good people at very little cost to you!"

Samme and Edith ran over to the group and stood beside the Baron. On seeing the girls the salesman looked even angrier. "I'm telling you all three to go home and attend to your own business." He doubled up his fist, all pretense of good nature gone. "There's plans afoot for the boy you figure owns this here cabin, which don't include livin' on this land nor running wild in the woods neither. They do include being caught and locked up . . . that's what. The sheriff will see to that and my cousin, Mrs. Dinliddy, will see he does his duty."

"Your cousin!" Edith stared at him. "So that's why she's pushing so hard to get Jason out of here. You two will sell Granny May's cabin and land and share the profits."

"Now, now," the salesman cried. "You girls are stickin' your nose in where you have no business. Gettin' yourselves all upset." Then he hurried off to join his retreating customers.

The Baron sputtered as he flung his battered hat on the ground. "I reckon we've done all there's to be done peacefully. There's just one thing left . . . shotgun justice."

"That's taking the law into your own. . . ." Edith started to say.

Samme broke in. "We won't give up." She pulled the Baron's sleeve. "Jason isn't caught. The cabin isn't sold."

"That talk's for ladies. I thank you for it." He raised his hat several times up and down above his head. "I'm off to get my firin' piece oiled." He stalked off at a fast pace.

"The Baron's sure stirred up, almost as much as I am," Samme said.

"No wonder, look!"

Samme looked. The cabin was getting a new roof of fresh oak shingles. Along the side in a pile lay the rotted broken shingles the Baron had replaced.

"A lot of hard work." Samme looked at the newly laid shingles. "Isn't the cabin beautiful? It's beginning to look like new. The Baron hoped he was fixing the cabin for Jason to live in. Now he thinks that salesman and Mrs. Dinliddy will get it. I'm worried about this shotgun justice thing, too." She turned to Edith.

"You keep a lookout," Edith ordered. "I'm going to call Jason out of the cave."

Samme took her post beyond the cabin. She heard two faint blasts on the horn as Edith leaned down into the trapdoor and blew. Samme knew the sound was traveling far underground along the narrow tunnels. She wanted to see Jason again yet dreaded telling him their bad news.

She waited for twenty minutes or so, then went into the cabin. The tall boy was just climbing out of the trapdoor. He listened, walked to the open door, stepped outside and kneeled down to place his ear to the earth. "Just to be sure there's no one walking about," he said. He looked with his far-seeing gaze across Summer Valley. "I heard the motor of a car on the main road."

"It was the salesman. He was here with some people. They just left."

The boy nodded and looked from one girl to the other. "What's the trouble?"

Edith gulped. "They're really serious about putting you in an orphanage. Even with the money for the taxes the law could still take you away. Aunt Rose will see about the worth of the jewelry—she will be taking it into town. We've come especially to tell you that the sheriff is putting a deputy on guard here at the cabin to catch you. Right away—tonight!"

To the girls' astonishment Jason began to laugh. "Haven't they been trying to catch me for a long time. If I wanted to I could stay hidden and live a comfortable life in the caves and woods." The boy's face became serious. He walked out the cabin door into the sun-sprinkled shade. "What I've learned in these years in the woods is that money isn't important, but the sun on my face is and seeing into the distant hills, clouds, rain, wind, they all matter, and people. You girls taught me that." Suddenly he raised his head, standing alert. "I hear voices from down the creek. Men—two men."

"I'll bet it's the sheriff," Samme declared, wide-eyed, "and the deputy."

"I'm going into the cave now," Jason said. He raised the trapdoor and slipped downward quietly. The girls stared at the rough gray boards.

Heavy footfalls and loud talk broke their silence. It was the sheriff. He nodded to the girls. "This is the cabin," he said to the lean fellow beside him. "You are to stay here until further notice or until the boy is found. If he shows up, grab him. At sundown I'll send a man to take your place." He turned to the girls in a fatherly manner. "You girls hike off home now. This is law business."

For Edith and Samme the walk home was even gloomier than the walk to the cabin.

15. TAKES ALL KINDS

Swiftly Friday came. Aunt Rose went to town, getting an early start. The girls were up—doing the chores had a soothing effect and helped the time to pass. They took the yellow corn from the loft over the black-and-white pig's pen, watching as the pig cracked the hard cobs, making the golden grains fall. They poured the cats a large pan of milk to heal their hurt feelings.

Edith stood up tall, looking over Summer Valley.

"What's all that commotion?" Samme stood beside her. "Who're all those people? There must be several dozen."

A crowd of men and women drew nearer. The women were dressed in assorted flowered prints and wearing sunbonnets. The men wore overalls and the soft felt hats of the hill men. There were the Henrys, whom the girls had met. The other people must also be neighbors they decided.

The leader, a lanky fellow with a weathered face, held out a long finger-marked paper. On the paper was a list of names.

His face and his whole appearance was of a man on a serious mission.

"Your aunt home?"

"She left a few minutes ago."

"Have something for you to tell her the minute she comes home." The leader waved the paper. "Need all the help we can get. We aim to add her name to this list." He pulled a wide wallet from his pocket as the rest of the people watched in nodding approval.

"We're collectin' money to save that boy's land and the cabin." He opened the wallet. Samme and Edith stared at the fat packet of worn bills. "We're covering the ridges, north, east, south and west. Folks is givin' generous, too. Tell your aunt we're feelin' bad how that woman, Mrs. Dinliddy, been tryin' to prod people into hunting out the boy. That boy has saved more sheep and calves lost in the back trails than we can count. We owe him this favor and much more for just the critters he's brought home."

"We think we should tell you," Edith spoke up. "Although we can't tell you just where—some money has been found that can be applied to paying the taxes on the May's land."

"That's some mighty good news to hear." The leader spoke for the gathering.

Another lanky man, with his hat between work-worn fists, stepped forward. " 'Twas he that found our lad aged three, when the little feller walked off last summer, durin' berry pickin'."

"It's the hermit boy brings Old Minnie herbs and roots, leavin' them on the back porch so's she can make her remedies and balms for the neighbors now that she cain't get around so spry," added a woman from the crowd.

"It's a serious business hauling a boy off from his friends," the leader said. "Tell your aunt not to be surprised if folks start comin' out this way with their shotguns in hand. We don't hanker to see that boy taken out of the hills, lessen he goes of his own free will."

The girls nodded.

"There's a meeting, early morning at the schoolhouse before the auction, your aunt will want to be there."

After quenching their thirst at the spring and some

talk among themselves the hill people moved off, still talking.

Edith put her hand to her forehead. "Can you beat that? The woods is full of people. Some trying to save Jason's land and some trying to take it. Some trying to catch him and some trying to leave him be."

"And I wonder," Samme said, "which group will win out."

The girls hurried back to the house, wondering what more could happen. They soon found out. There came a remembered clanking sound. Edith finished pushing two sticks of wood into the iron cooking stove, replaced the iron lid and hurried to the door.

"I thought I remembered that sound," Samme squealed. "I can't see it. Must have parked out on the county road. I could bet on it. That's Henry's old truck. The truck that needs so much water! Remember."

"How could I forget," Edith smiled. "But what would he be doing out here now?"

"We will know in fifteen or twenty minutes." Samme positioned herself at the door to watch. "If Henry could have brought us by the new county road way instead of by the old house way we might not have had to get our feet so wet."

"True!" Edith added. "But we might just have got ourselves lost in the woods walking from the road to Aunt Rose's house! We were dudes those days."

"Now we are almost experienced hillsmen," Samme boasted.

And there he was. The same old dusty Henry, stopping at the spring.

"Look," Samme laughed, pointing. "He has the same fruit juice can. The truck's drinking cup."

"There's men behind him." Edith peered down the path through the tree limbs. "All of them are coming to the house."

Henry greeted the girls happily.

"Brought you some news fellers out." He grinned. "Now don't let this go to your heads, girls, didn't bring them to see you!"

By now the newsmen had caught up with Henry and taken over the conversation. One was carrying a camera. "Hello there, girls. You folks live the closest! We came to find out more about that wild hermit boy who hides out here in the woods. This story is making national news. Got wind, too, that his granny's cabin is about to be sold. That ought to bring him out of hiding."

"Yes, sir." The other newsman looked away into the thick forests. "The storekeeper tells us the hill folks are collecting money. Says they may be showing up with shotguns. A regular uprising, all on account of this kid saving their lambs. Takes all kinds!"

Henry went to the spring to carry water for his faithful truck.

"Since all this hubbub about the hermit boy started we knew we'd have to come out here. Henry led the way in that old truck. Hired him in town." The tallest newsman talked on. "Said he brought you girls out here a while back. Cost five bucks him showing us the way, but it's going to pay off. Sheriff told us about where the cabin's located. We'll be back, girls."

"Just going to get a few pictures of that empty cabin," the cameraman said. "Maybe we'll see the hermit kid, too. Sure hope he's got real long hair, look good on the front page."

"You think he'll be wearing a leopardskin suit?" The newsman started off laughing.

"Not much chance of them surprising Jason," Samme observed.

"Henry's gone off to the county road, watering that truck," Edith said. She took the potatoes off the stove. There came the sound of women's voices. "More people," Edith said.

"What a day." Samme looked out the door. "Oh, oh, she's here again—Mrs. Dinliddy."

Three women were approaching the house. The overpowering Mrs. Dinliddy was in the lead. Two fashionably dressed women, each carrying a briefcase, followed. The girls, mindful of Aunt Rose's instructions not to ask Mrs. Dinliddy inside, walked outdoors to meet them.

"Aren't these two fine examples of adorable backwoods children," cooed a woman who was wearing a red suit. She smiled at the girls and fussed around in the case she carried until she came up with a bag of lemon drops.

"Don't let them fool you," Mrs. Dinliddy said. "They're just as sly as their aunt and set to take advantage of any townspeople that come their way."

The lady in red pushed a bag of lemon drops into

Samme's hand. "There now. Haven't had any of those in a long while have you? She's a regular little 'Girl of the Limberlost,' wouldn't you say, Mabel?"

Mabel wouldn't say or didn't have a chance, for Mrs. Dinliddy spoke up.

"Now, girls, let's have some cooperation here, pay attention and do as these ladies ask."

The lady in red, whose name was Mildred, spoke. "Girls, we are here on a mission of mercy." She paused as if to give the girls time to let this idea sink in. "A poor lonely frightened boy lives hidden away in this great wilderness. We want an interview with him for our magazine, *Lady's Day.* You want to help him? Of course you do. When our dear readers hear about him, they'll send him all kinds of nice things. Just think of that. Sweets, clothing, books." She smiled down on the girls and patted Samme's head.

"Sorry we can't help," both girls sang out.

"See! Didn't I warn you," Mrs. Dinliddy cried, vexed. "It's shades of their aunt they are. Molly-coddling won't soften them up and your lemon drops are as good as wasted. Never mind them. We will find the boy ourselves if we have to upturn every stump and prod every mine hole and flush out every attic in these hills."

She stamped off, the other two women followed. The girls closed the door, grinning. "Those magazine ladies did seem real nice," Samme said, addressing the bean pot. "It's just they were in bad company. I have this peculiar feeling there's going to be someone lost in the woods today for sure and I don't mean Jason."

Edith nodded, agreeing.

The girls were thankful by the time their Aunt Rose returned that all was quiet. Aunt Rose set her town hat on the polished table and propped her large purse beside it. "I have good news," she said. "And bad news, too." She looked inquiringly at the waiting girls. "Which will you have first?"

"I suppose you may as well break the bad news first," Edith said soberly.

"The jewelry isn't worth enough to pay the rest of the tax money. Better news is that I had a long talk with someone special and more good news." Here Aunt Rose reached into her purse bringing out a slip of paper with writing on it. "I have the address of a natural history museum that might be interested in Jason's cave relics."

Samme brought her hands together softly. "Oh gee, Aunt Rose, that is good news."

"And we have news for you, too," Edith said. "But I'm not sure if it's good or bad. A crowd of your neighbors from around the hills were here. They are collecting money among themselves to help Jason."

"And tomorrow morning there is to be a meeting at the schoolhouse before the auction." The girls told about the magazine women and right off the mention of Mrs. Dinliddy's name brought a frown.

It was after dark by the time supper had been eaten. They soon made ready for bed, tomorrow would be a busy day.

"Good night, girls," Aunt Rose said. "I did hope we

might be able to save the land, perhaps there is a way to save Jason, too."

"What does she mean by that?" Samme whispered.

Just after daylight they were awakened by someone banging on the door. There stood Henry again, with an excited stranger. Henry looked as if he were sorry to have arrived at such an hour, but the stranger had only his own problems on his mind.

"You people seem to live the closest to the cabin where that wild boy's grandma used to live, so this fellow says."

Aunt Rose stiffened.

"I want to wrap up that story about the boy before the Kansas City papers get wind of it. Sent two of my best men out here yesterday along with a cameraman. They haven't returned nor called, nor sent a word of copy."

Aunt Rose's mouth set in a tight line. Noting her sour face, the early morning visitor drew a card from his wallet. "City editor, ma'am, *Brown City Times*. See anything of two newsmen and a cameraman? They were to return to the city last night. They've never had an assignment in the hills before. Not many hermit boys around to write about. . . ."

Aunt Rose shoved the card back into the talking man's hand. "That's for your interferin' newsmen and your cameraman. And you, too," she added as an afterthought. "Dern fools are likely roamin' the woods lost this minute."

The editor of the *Brown City Times* looked off over Summer Valley, seeing the endless forests that rimmed it on every side. "But could three grown men get lost?" He turned to Henry with the question.

"Three could get lost, same as one," Henry answered. "Lived here most all my life and can just barely find my way in and out."

Aunt Rose stood stiff and unhospitable. "Good thing I didn't catch them on this property. My nieces told me those fellows were along here yesterday. How they could disappear between here and Granny May's cabin is more than I can figure. They have no business chasin' that boy. It's all bound to end up in mischief or worse."

She drew Samme and Edith into the house and slammed the door.

They heard the editor say to Henry, "Take me over to that cabin. Don't leave my side for a minute . . . and don't get lost. Maybe we can find those reporters."

The two men struck off into the woods.

16. LAW OF THE LAND

Samme and Edith couldn't help wondering what had become of the two women from *Lady's Day*, the ones who had come to get a story on the hermit boy for their magazine and Mrs. Dinliddy.

"What's a 'Girl of the Limberlost'?" Samme asked her sister. "Those women said we looked just like that."

"They were just trying to butter us up," Edith laughed. " 'The Girl of the Limberlost' is a story about a girl who lived out in a wild woodsy country like this."

"I still have their lemon drops," Samme said.

"Let me have one."

Aunt Rose was grumbling over by the stove and making a lot of racket with the lifter and the iron lids. "It's a bigger crowd than we have at a barn-raising or a holiday pie supper. I'm that upset I can't concentrate on hoeing in the garden. The weeds will take over and I shall starve next winter. It'll all be on the heads of these folks from the city."

The girls were dressed and were just sitting down to breakfast when the most awful bellowing came from down along the creek. The sun had just come up strong with the beginnings of a beautiful day. They ran out the door.

There was quite a crowd of active, noisy people at the spring.

At first the girls thought it was the group of hill neighbors again. But there were no women in the crowd and a second look proved these to be all strangers.

It was a group of men trailing dogs on leashes.

"Bloodhounds for trackin'," Aunt Rose declared over the girls' shoulders.

"Tracking what?" Samme asked.

"If they're doing what I fear they are doing, they've gone too far," Aunt Rose declared, going into the house.

Before the girls realized what she was up to, Aunt Rose returned with a wicked-looking and very long muzzled shotgun.

"She's loaded and ready to fire," Aunt Rose declared. "It appears as if the showdown has come and I wish my neighbors were at my side, but as they aren't, I'll go it alone."

The half-dozen men with as many dogs on leashes and a bevy of helpers looked toward the house. Seeing the two girls and an angry woman with a shotgun, they huddled together as if deciding something. A burly fellow then separated from the huddle and came up the path. He put his hand out as a signal for peace and managed to pull off his hunting cap at the same time.

"Howdy, ma'am. No harm intended, just resting a bit. Been sent in to hunt three ladies that are missing. Mrs. Dinliddy and two magazine writer ladies who have strayed off and got lost. Sure hope we catch a look at that hermit boy that is said to hole up somewhere in these hills. Papers are full of it. Good day, ma'am."

Aunt Rose lowered the shotgun.

"She thought they were going to use those hounds to track down Jason," Edith whispered to Samme.

"Whatever trouble they get into is their just deserts," Aunt Rose said disgustedly. "More city folks in the hills these days than there are in town."

"They went thataway," Samme called after the burly man.

When Aunt Rose was dressed to start for the meeting at the schoolhouse she took up her purse and laid a sealed envelope on the table. "I have something very important for you girls to do," she said. "In fact you are the only ones who can do the job."

"We will always do what we can to help," Edith said. Samme nodded.

"You must get this envelope to Jason May before the auction!" Aunt Rose hurried out the door.

"What are we waiting for?" Samme took up the envelope. "What do you suppose is so important about this letter?"

"I'm not sure," Edith said. "But we can trust Aunt Rose. We will have to get this message to Jason through the trapdoor in Granny May's cabin."

"The deputy is going to be on guard," Samme said.

"I know." Edith set the last dish in the cupboard and wiped the tabletop. "We'll have to get there before the auction crowd overruns the place. There will be a big crowd. So much has been written about Jason in the papers and passed by word of mouth. People are curious about him."

"Yes! People from the city think of the Ozarks as one huge picnic ground. There will be whole families with their lunch hampers and maybe even the family dog."

"The biggest problem is getting past that deputy," Edith said thoughtfully. She took a small candle, some matches and put them in her pocket along with the envelope with the message enclosed for Jason.

"Hurry!" Samme urged. "What do you think of this plan to get the deputy's attention?" She asked as they hurried along. The girls talked back and forth earnestly until they reached Granny May's cabin.

The deputy leaned against a pig-nut hickory, whistling back and forth with a blue jay perched just overhead.

"Hello," Samme said.

"Hello." The deputy smiled. "Aren't you girls a little early for the auction?"

"Just wanted a good seat." Edith went to the cabin door.

"Oh." The deputy resumed his whistling with the jay.

Samme tugged his sleeve.

"What you want?" The deputy gave Samme his full attention.

Edith stepped inside the cabin door.

"I'm thirsty," Samme said.

"There's the spring." The deputy pointed down the hill.

"Would you go with me?" Samme pleaded. "I'm afraid."

"How come?"

"There's a snake down there." Samme noted Edith was now over the trapdoor.

"There's no snake down there." The deputy peered down the hill at the pool of tree-reflecting water.

"There was the other day," Samme sniffed. She was glad this was true, for she felt just a little wicked. "I saw it, a big fat copperhead snake lying there— sunning on the rocks right by the spring. Won't you go down with me and scare the snake away? You know there will be city folks coming to the auction." Samme rolled her eyes. "If one of those city folks was to be bitten, it would be part your fault 'cause you didn't go down there with me and scare the snake away. The sheriff wouldn't like that."

"Aw shucks!" The deputy unwound his legs where he was all relaxed against the tree. "Well, O.K. But you better wait here. I'll bring you a drink. No use takin' any chances."

"Oh no, sir," Samme said and looked at Edith. "No use taking any chances."

"I'll just go kick around at those rocks a bit and bring us both a cold drink. How's that?"

"Perfect, just perfect," Samme cried.

With the deputy kicking rocks around at the spring it was a simple task to take down the horn from the rafter, lift the trapdoor, light the candle and lay the envelope beside the lighted candle so the hermit boy would be certain to see the message. Edith leaned into the trapdoor and blew on the horn, closed the trapdoor and laid the horn back on the rafter.

All this in seconds before the deputy running full speed, his container of water sloshing at every step made it to the top of the hill. "You girls hear that sound?" He was looking every which way.

"Sort of a muffled blast."

Puffing, he handed the water to Samme. "Back fire on the county road I 'spect. Nothing to worry about."

"No, sir." Samme smiled. "Nothing to worry about. Thank you for the water."

"I gave those snakes a good stirrin'," the deputy said.

The crowd soon began to gather. Country folks, city folks and strangers. They came in flocks like brightly plumed birds, chattering. Gaily dressed people of assorted ages milled about. Scattered under trees were folding chairs, hampers, blankets, sleeping bags and even scattered tents.

A fat baby in nylon crawlers sat at the edge of his blanket sticking pebbles in his mouth. The auctioneer stepped up on a stump and called out the rules of the sale. The Grove girls were taking a steady flow of dimes by selling lemonade made from the icy water of the spring. The Ladies Club of Rough Gulch offered coffee and homemade pie and rummage at bargain prices, the profits to go for the missions to uplift destitute Australian aborigines.

The sheriff stood in the door of Granny May's cabin with a cross look on his face. His shouts tried to rise above the hubbub. He pleaded with the people who were just sightseers to go home.

"Have enough lost out here already!" he shouted.

"I'm staying to see that hermit boy captured," shrilled a woman.

"I'll bet he kicks and bites," another shouted.

"We've come three hundred miles just to see the hermit boy, so we're staying," a voice called.

"Me, too." "Us, too." "My family, too," came from the crowd.

"Read about it in the paper," shouted someone else.

"Haven't nary a track of the hermit boy," the sheriff shouted back. "If it's his capture you're waiting on, I say head for home."

"No, no." "Never," people shouted from the crowd.

The sheriff stepped into the yard. He placed his large foot into a melted, clinging mound of toasted marshmallow. He teetered back and forth, standing on one leg, scraping his shoe with a twig. The color of his face changed from red to purple. The greedy salesman hurried over to prop him up.

"Bad day, eh, Sheriff?"

The sheriff grunted.

"I have the money right here to buy the cabin. Nice property if I do say so myself. Might be you may want to buy it off me someday yourself, Sheriff."

"Shut up!" growled the sheriff.

"You got your duty to do," whined the salesman. "My cousin, poor Mrs. Dinliddy, lost out in the deep woods. She may never be seen again."

"There's a fresh brace of bloodhounds being brought into the hunt for your cousin, Mrs. Dinliddy, and those magazine writer women," growled the sheriff.

The sheriff turned his back. "No, lady," he said to a

woman who was pounding on his shoulder. "No trace of the hermit boy yet."

The sheriff shouted until he was hoarse. Then he went to where Old Minnie had set up a stand on a wee stump. She was doing a brisk business selling Black Cherry Bark throat balm. He swallowed some and made a terrible face.

"I needed that!" he gasped, and began shouting again.

A girl in a miniskirt called above the crowd, "How long did you say his hair was, Sheriff?" Then she ran off giggling with her friends. The sheriff scratched his head.

"My two boys are lost and gone!" cried a father.

"Just berry-picking. No cause to worry I'm sure," said the sheriff.

"No cause to worry!" cried the father. "That's the very place those bears hide out . . . behind berry bushes!"

The sheriff was busy holding off a child who was trying to get a grip on his pocket pistol.

"I want that Boom-Boom," wailed the child, jumping up and down.

A large woman, the child's mother, faced the sheriff. "Mean, selfish old man," she hissed. "Mama's Itsy Bitsy can't have mean man's Boom-Boom," she told the child.

Itsy Bitsy fell screaming on the grass.

"Been huntin' you, Sheriff." It was the auctioneer.

"Better get some order in this crowd. The auction starts in five minutes."

"Five minutes!" Samme gasped.

"He's going to call the auction in five minutes and the hill folks from the meeting aren't here yet to help Jason."

The girls moved in next to the auctioneer. "Something will have to be done to delay the auction," Edith whispered.

The auctioneer looked at his watch.

"What's holding up the auction?" the salesman demanded.

"Five minutes is up," the sheriff said.

The auctioneer stepped up on the stump.

The girls had their head together, whispering.

"Get on with it," the salesman gritted.

"Stop! Wait!" Samme cried.

"Hold the auction," Edith called.

"Quiet." The salesman fumed.

"The terms of this here auction will be cash," the auctioneer shouted.

The salesman waved a handful of money.

"Let me speak," Edith cried.

"Time's wasting," the salesman grumbled.

"I said," roared the sheriff over the other sounds, "let the young lady speak her piece."

"Thank goodness," Edith said.

"Is that all you have to say?" demanded the sheriff.

"No, sir!" Edith cried. "The hill folks are coming!"

"The hill folks are coming, hurrah! hurrah!" Samme sang.

Sure enough the hill folks from the meeting were coming over the top of the rise, moving to the scene of the battle. Aunt Rose and the Baron were leading the charge. The crowd cleared a path as the auctioneer took the stump.

"Gather 'round! Gather 'round!" he called. Excitement ran through the crowd.

The Baron lifted his hat to the girls.

"Are we glad to see you, Aunt Rose," Samme sighed.

"Let me have the stump," Aunt Rose said. "I have a few words to say."

"I'll never get on with this sale." The auctioneer complained.

"Let her speak!" the sheriff roared.

The hill folks stood in close. The men hats in hand. The women peering from under calico poke bonnets. The children peeking from around their mothers' skirts.

"You all knew Granny May," Aunt Rose said.

There was a murmur of assent among the people.

"Yea, for Granny May," a picnicker cried. The crowd took up the chant. "Yea!" "Yea!" "Yea!"

"You all know her grandson, Jason, called by some the hermit boy of Summer Valley." At the mention of Jason's name a great cry of approval went up. "You all know the good works Jason has done for each of you."

Bare heads and bonnets nodded.

"Now I want everyone to know that the hill folks

have done something special for their friend, Jason," Aunt Rose said. "Here, Sheriff, this money was brought together by all the good hill folks who are friends and neighbors of Jason and think he is the finest young man ever was!"

"Bah!" The salesman turned away.

The sheriff, looking pleased and relieved, counted the money rapidly. "There isn't enough here," he cried distressedly.

"Ha," the salesman said.

"Come here, girls." Aunt Rose drew the girls close. She thrust the leather pouch into their hands. "You found Jason so in a way you found this money, too. Give the pouch to the sheriff. This will make up the difference, Sheriff.

"Now." She addressed the gathering. "I want you all to meet Edith and Samme, who sought the boy, Jason, for only one reason, to be friends. They of all the seekers were successful, so may I present you my nieces, the girls who found the hermit boy of Summer Valley. Edith and Samme."

The crowd cheered, throwing up hats and waving handkerchiefs. The girls placed the leather pouch in the sheriff's hands.

Again the sheriff counted rapidly. "Enough! Enough!" he cried. "The cabin is saved."

There was a snort. The salesman slipped away through the crowd.

"I do have a few more words," Aunt Rose said.

"Speak up," cried the sheriff in good humor.

"Because of these two girls the hermit boy is with us today," Aunt Rose said.

"Where! Where!" shouted the crowd.

A hush fell over the crowd. The hermit boy himself stood outlined in the door of the cabin. For once the crowd remained quiet, opening a path for the hermit boy to pass until he stood by Aunt Rose and the girls. In his hands he held the envelope the girls had placed beneath the trapdoor.

The sheriff took Jason's arm. "The taxes are paid," he said. "The cabin and the land are saved but—I shall have to take the boy. I'm very sorry but that is the law of the land. Boy can't be allowed to roam homeless. He needs care."

"Have you opened the envelope?" Aunt Rose asked Jason.

"Yes, ma'am," Jason said.

"Do you agree?"

"Yes," Jason said.

"There you are, Sheriff," Aunt Rose said. "You can let go of the boy. Jason May has just agreed to me being his legal guardian. I had papers made up and signed by the judge in town. Those papers are right here in my purse. The envelope in Jason's hand is a note asking if he would be agreeable. Now Jason will stay here in the hills where he belongs, and that's according to the law of the land, too, Sheriff."

"This is one time I don't mind being bested." The sheriff shook Jason's hand. "Glad to see you with us again, son."

"Thank you, sir," Jason replied.

"Finish up your picnic lunches, folks, and go home. Hey! Wait just a minute," cried the sheriff. "I can't go home. Too many lost ones still out here in the woods." He looked at the hermit boy.

"The women," Jason said, "are roaming around among the buildings in the old town of Winkler. I've noticed the birds circling restlessly in that area. The men have blundered into the hillside entrance to the cave. I heard their voices. The tunnel they are sitting in is only a few hundred yards from the entrance, but they don't know that. If you'll just send some men with a light to lead them out."

"Come along, girls, come along, Jason," Aunt Rose said and all four started down the path towards Aunt Rose's house. Aunt Rose walked a way, then stopped. "What's that hammering?" she asked the girls.

"You were too busy to notice, Aunt Rose," Samme said. "The Baron climbed right upon the cabin and started laying shingles, to finish fixing the roof of Jason's cabin the minute the sheriff said the taxes were paid."

"You have all been so good," Jason said as they continued down the path. "What can I ever do to repay everyone's kindness?"

"Just stay in Summer Valley always, Jason," Edith said.

"And teach us all about the woods when we come here in the summers," Samme added.

They walked in silence until they reached Aunt Rose's house.

"Jason," Aunt Rose said, thoughtfully, "I have the

address—if you wish you can write to the natural history museum people. They will be interested in your cave and the relics."

"I do want to share the treasures," Jason said. "Mine and Granny's. Thank you for everything. May I call you Aunt Rose?"

"Please do, Jason," Aunt Rose said and her eyes were moist.

She opened the door. Edith and Samme and Jason walked into the house. Aunt Rose followed, closing the door softly behind her.